Pipefuls

Christopher Morley

Pipefuls

The present edition is a reproduction of previous publication of this classic work. Minor typographical errors may have been corrected without note; however, for an authentic reading experience the spelling, punctuation, and capitalization have been retained from the original text.

ISBN: 978-1-64799-687-1

THIS BOOK IS DEDICATED

TO

THREE MEN

HULBERT FOOTNER

EUGENE SAXTON

WILLIAM ROSE BENÉT

BECAUSE, IF I MENTIONED ONLY ONE

OF THEM, I WOULD HAVE TO

WRITE BOOKS

TO INSCRIBE TO THE OTHER TWO

CONTENTS

Tales of Two Cities
I
Philadelphia

II
New York

PREFACE

Sir Thomas Browne said that Eve was "edified out of the rib of Adam." This little book was edified (for the most part) out of the ribs of two friendly newspapers, The New York Evening Post and The Philadelphia Evening Public Ledger. To them, and to The Bookman, Everybody's, and The Publishers' Weekly, I am grateful for permission to reprint.

Tristram Shandy said, "When a man is hemm'd in by two indecorums, and must commit one of 'em let him chuse which he will, the world will blame him." Now it is one indecorum to let this collection of small sketches go out (as they do) unrevised and just as they assaulted the defenceless reader of the daily prints; and the other indecorum would be to take fragments of this kind too gravely, and attempt by more careful disposition of their pallid members to arrange them into some appearance of painless decease. As Gilbert Chesterton said (I wish I could say, on a similar occasion): "Their vices are too vital to be improved with a blue pencil, or with anything I can think of, except dynamite."

These sketches gave me pain to write; they will give the judicious patron pain to read; therefore we are quits. I think, as I look over their slattern paragraphs, of that most tragic hour—it falls about 4 p. m. in the office of an evening newspaper—when the unhappy compiler tries to round up the broodings of the day and still get home in time for supper. And yet perhaps the will-to-live is in them, for are they not a naked exhibit of the antics a man will commit in order to earn a living? In extenuation it may be pleaded that none of them are so long that they may not be mitigated by an accompanying pipe of tobacco.

THE AUTHOR
Roslyn, Long Island,
July, 1920

ON MAKING FRIENDS

Considering that most friendships are made by mere hazard, how is it that men find themselves equipped and fortified with just the friends they need? We have heard of men who asserted that they would like to have more money, or more books, or more pairs of pyjamas; but we have never heard of a man saying that he did not have enough friends. For, while one can never have too many friends, yet those one has are always enough. They satisfy us completely. One has never met a man who would say, "I wish I had a friend who would combine the good humour of A, the mystical enthusiasm of B, the love of doughnuts which is such an endearing quality in C, and who would also have the habit of giving Sunday evening suppers like D, and the well-stocked cellar which is so deplorably lacking in E." No; the curious thing is that at any time and in any settled way of life a man is generally provided with friends far in excess of his desert, and also in excess of his capacity to absorb their wisdom and affectionate attentions.

There is some pleasant secret behind this, a secret that none is wise enough to fathom. The infinite fund of disinterested humane kindliness that is adrift in the world is part of the riddle, the insoluble riddle of life that is born in our blood and tissue. It is agreeable to think that no man, save by his own gross fault, ever went through life unfriended, without companions to whom he could stammer his momentary impulses of sagacity, to whom he could turn in hours of loneliness. It is not even necessary to know a man to be his friend. One can sit at a lunch counter, observing the moods and whims of the white-coated pie-passer, and by the time you have juggled a couple of fried eggs you will have caught some grasp of his philosophy of life, seen the quick edge and tang of his humour, memorized the shrewdness of his worldly insight and been as truly stimulated as if you had spent an evening with your favourite parson.

If there were no such thing as friendship existing to-day, it would perhaps be difficult to understand what it is like from those who have written about it. We have tried, from time to time, to read Emerson's enigmatic and rather frigid essay. It seems that Emerson must have put his cronies to a severe test before admitting them to the high-vaulted and rather draughty halls of his intellect. There are fine passages in his essay, but it is intellectualized, bloodless, heedless of the trifling oddities of human intercourse that make friendship so satisfying. He seems to insist upon a sterile ceremony

1

of mutual self-improvement, a kind of religious ritual, a profound interchange of doctrines between soul and soul. His friends (one gathers) are to be antisepticated, all the poisons and pestilence of their faulty humours are to be drained away before they may approach the white and icy operating table of his heart. "Why insist," he says, "on rash personal relations with your friend? Why go to his house, or know his wife and family?" And yet does not the botanist like to study the flower in the soil where it grows?

Polonius, too, is another ancient supposed to be an authority on friendship. The Polonius family must have been a thoroughly dreary one to live with; we have often thought that poor Ophelia would have gone mad anyway, even if there had been no Hamlet. Laertes preaches to Ophelia; Polonius preaches to Laertes. Laertes escaped by going abroad, but the girl had to stay at home. Hamlet saw that pithy old Polonius was a preposterous and orotund ass. Polonius's doctrine of friendship—"The friends thou hast, and their adoption tried, grapple them to thy soul with hoops of steel"—was, we trow, a necessary one in his case. It would need a hoop of steel to keep them near such a dismal old sawmonger.

Friendships, we think, do not grow up in any such carefully tended and contemplated fashion as Messrs. Emerson and Polonius suggest. They begin haphazard. As we look back on the first time we saw our friends we find that generally our original impression was curiously astray. We have worked along beside them, have consorted with them drunk or sober, have grown to cherish their delicious absurdities, have outrageously imposed on each other's patience—and suddenly we awoke to realize what had happened. We had, without knowing it, gained a new friend. In some curious way the unseen border line had been passed. We had reached the final culmination of Anglo-Saxon regard when two men rarely look each other straight in the eyes because they are ashamed to show each other how fond they are. We had reached the fine flower and the ultimate test of comradeship—that is, when you get a letter from one of your "best friends," you know you don't need to answer it until you get ready to.

Emerson is right in saying that friendship can't be hurried. It takes time to ripen. It needs a background of humorous, wearisome, or even tragic events shared together, a certain tract of memories shared in common, so that you know that your own life and your companion's have really moved for some time in the same channel. It needs interchange of books, meals together, discussion of one another's whims with mutual friends, to gain a proper perspective.

2

It is set in a rich haze of half-remembered occasions, sudden glimpses, ludicrous pranks, unsuspected observations, midnight confidences when heart spoke to candid heart.

The soul preaches humility to itself when it realizes, startled, that it has won a new friend. Knowing what a posset of contradictions we all are, it feels a symptom of shame at the thought that our friend knows all our frailties and yet thinks us worth affection. We all have cause to be shamefast indeed; for whereas we love ourselves in spite of our faults, our friends often love us even on account of our faults, the highest level to which attachment can go. And what an infinite appeal there is in their faces! How we grow to cherish those curious little fleshy cages—so oddly sculptured—which inclose the spirit within. To see those faces, bent unconsciously over their tasks—each different, each unique, each so richly and queerly expressive of the lively and perverse enigma of man, is a full education in human tolerance. Privately, one studies his own ill-modeled visnomy to see if by any chance it bespeaks the emotions he inwardly feels. We know—as Hamlet did—the vicious mole of nature in us, the o'ergrowth of some complexion that mars the purity of our secret resolutions. Yet—our friends have passed it over, have shown their willingness to take us as we are. Can we do less than hope to deserve their generous tenderness, granted before it was earned?

The problem of education, said R. L. S., is two-fold—"first to know, then to utter." Every man knows what friendship means, but few can utter that complete frankness of communion, based upon full comprehension of mutual weakness, enlivened by a happy understanding of honourable intentions generously shared. When we first met our friends we met with bandaged eyes. We did not know what journeys they had been on, what winding roads their spirits had travelled, what ingenious shifts they had devised to circumvent the walls and barriers of the world. We know these now, for some of them they have told us; others we have guessed. We have watched them when they little dreamed it; just as they (we suppose) have done with us. Every gesture and method of their daily movement have become part of our enjoyment of life. Not until a time comes for saying good-bye will we ever know how much we would like to have said. At those times one has to fall back on shrewder tongues. You remember Hilaire Belloc:

From quiet homes and first beginning
Out to the undiscovered ends,
There's nothing worth the wear of winning
But laughter, and the love of friends.

3

THOUGHTS ON CIDER

Our friend Dove Dulcet, the poet, came into our kennel and found us arm in arm with a deep demijohn of Chester County cider. We poured him out a beaker of the cloudy amber juice. It was just in prime condition, sharpened with a blithe tingle, beaded with a pleasing bubble of froth. Dove looked upon it with a kindled eye. His arm raised the tumbler in a manner that showed this gesture to be one that he had compassed before. The orchard nectar began to sluice down his throat.

Dove is one who has faced many and grievous woes. His Celtic soul peers from behind cloudy curtains of alarm. Old unhappy far-off things and battles long ago fume in the smoke of his pipe. His girded spirit sees agrarian unrest in the daffodil and industrial riot in a tin of preserved prunes. He sees the world moving on the brink of horror and despair. Sweet dalliance with a baked bloater on a restaurant platter moves him to grief over the hard lot of the Newfoundland fishing fleet. Six cups of tea warm him to anguish over the peonage of Sir Thomas Lipton's coolies in Ceylon. Souls in perplexity cluster round him like Canadian dimes in a cash register in Plattsburgh, N. Y. He is a human sympathy trust. When we are on our deathbed we shall send for him. The perfection of his gentle sorrow will send us roaring out into the dark, and will set a valuable example to the members of our family.

But it is the rack of clouds that makes the sunset lovely. The bosomy vapours of Dove's soul are the palette upon which the decumbent sun of his spirit casts its vivid orange and scarlet colours. His joy is the more perfect to behold because it bursts goldenly through the pangs of his tender heart. His soul is like the infant Moses, cradled among dark and prickly bullrushes; but anon it floats out upon the river and drifts merrily downward on a sparkling spate.

It has nothing to do with Dove, but we will here interject the remark that a pessimist overtaken by liquor is the cheeriest sight in the world. Who is so extravagantly, gloriously, and irresponsibly gay?

Dove's eyes beaconed as the cider went its way. The sweet lingering tang filled the arch of his palate with a soft mellow cheer. His gaze fell upon us as his head tilted gently backward. We wish there had been a painter there—someone like F. Walter Taylor—to rush onto canvas the gorgeous benignity of his aspect. It would have been a portrait of the rich Flemish school. Dove's eyes were full of a tender emotion, mingled with a charmed and wistful surprise. It was as though the poet was saying he had not realized there was anything so good left on earth. His bearing was devout, religious, mystical. In one moment of revelation (so it appeared to us as we watched) Dove looked upon all the profiles and aspects of life, and found them of noble outline. Not since the grandest of Grand Old Parties went out of power has Dove looked less as though he felt the world were on the verge of an abyss. For several moments revolution and anarchy receded, profiteers were tamed, capital and labour purred together on a mattress of catnip, and the cosmos became a free verse poem. He did not even utter the customary and ungracious remark of those to whom cider potations are given: "That'll be at its best in about a week." We apologized for the cider being a little warmish from standing (discreetly hidden) under our desk. Douce man, he said: "I think cider, like ale, ought not to be drunk too cold. I like it just this way." He stood for a moment, filled with theology and metaphysics. "By gracious," he said, "it makes all the other stuff taste like poison." Still he stood for a brief instant, transfixed with complete bliss. It was apparent to us that his mind was busy with apple orchards and autumn sunshine. Perhaps he was wondering whether he could make a poem out of it. Then he turned softly and went back to his job in a life insurance office.

As for ourself, we then poured out another tumbler, lit a corncob pipe, and meditated. Falstaff once said that he had forgotten what the inside of a church looked like. There will come a time when many of us will perhaps have forgotten what the inside of a saloon looked like, but there will still be the consolation of the cider jug. Like the smell of roasting chestnuts and the comfortable equatorial warmth of an oyster stew, it is a consolation hard to put into words. It calls irresistibly for tobacco; in fact the true cider toper always pulls a long puff at his pipe before each drink, and blows some of the smoke into the glass so that he gulps down some of the blue reek with his draught. Just why this should be, we know not. Also some enthusiasts insist on having small sugared cookies with their cider; others cry loudly for Reading pretzels. Some have ingenious theories about letting the jug stand, either tightly stoppered or else unstoppered, until it becomes "hard." In our experience hard cider is distressingly like drinking vinegar. We prefer it soft, with all its sweetness and the transfusing savour of the fruit animating it. At the peak of its deliciousness it has a small, airy sparkle against the roof of the mouth, a delicate tactile sensation like the feet of dancing flies. This, we presume, is the 4½ to 7 per cent of sin with which fermented cider is credited by works of reference. There are pedants and bigots who insist that the jug must be stoppered with a corncob. For our own part, the stopper does not stay in the neck long enough after the demijohn reaches us to make it worth while worrying about this matter. Yet a nice attention to detail may prove that the cob has some secret affinity with cider, for a Missouri meerschaum never tastes so well as after three glasses of this rustic elixir.

That ingenious student of social niceties, John Mistletoe, in his famous Dictionary of Deplorable Facts—a book which we heartily commend to the curious, for he includes a long and most informing article on cider, tracing its etymology from the old Hebrew word shaker meaning "to quaff deeply"—maintains that cider should only be drunk beside an open fire of applewood logs:

> And preferably on an evening of storm and wetness, when
> the swish and sudden pattering of rain against the panes
> lend an added agreeable snugness to the cheerful scene
> within, where master and dame sit by the rosy hearth
> frying sausages in a pan laid on the embers.

This reminds one of the anecdote related by ex-Senator Beveridge in his Life of John Marshall. Justice Story told his wife that the justices of the Supreme Court were of a self-denying habit, never taking wine except in wet weather. "But it does sometimes happen that the Chief Justice will say to me, when the cloth is removed, 'Brother Story, step to the window and see if it does not look like rain.' And if I tell him that the sun is shining brightly, Judge Marshall will sometimes reply, 'All the better, for our jurisdiction extends over so large a territory that the doctrine of chances makes it certain that it must be raining somewhere.'"

Our own theory about cider is that the time to drink it is when it reaches you; and if it hails from Chester County, so much the better.

We remember with gusto a little soliloquy on cider delivered by another friend of ours, as we both stood in a decent ordinary on Fulton Street, going through all the motions of jocularity and cheer. Cider (he said) is our refuge and strength. Cider, he insisted, drawing from his pocket a clipping much tarnished with age, is a drink for men of reason and genteel nurture; a drink for such as desire to drink pleasantly, amiably, healthily, and with perseverance and yet retain the command and superintendence of their faculties. I have here (he continued) a clipping sent me by an eminent architect in the great city of Philadelphia (a city which it is a

6

pleasure for me to contemplate by reason of the beauty and virtue of its women, the infinite vivacity and good temper of its men, the rectitudinal disposition of its highways)—I have here (he exclaimed) a clipping sent me by an architect of fame, charming parts, and infinite cellarage, explaining the virtues of cider. Cider, this clipping asserts, produces a clearness of the complexion. It brightens the eye, particularly in women, conducing to the composition of generous compliment and all the social suavity that endears the intercourse of the sexes. Longevity, this extract maintains, is the result of application to good cider. The Rev. Martin Johnson, vicar of Dilwyn, in Herefordshire, from 1651 to 1698 (he read from his clipping), wrote:

> This parish, wherein sider is plentiful, hath many people that do enjoy this blessing of long life; neither are the aged bedridden or decrepit as elsewhere; next to God, wee ascribe it to our flourishing orchards, first that the bloomed trees in spring do not only sweeten but purify the ambient air; next, that they yield us plenty of rich and winy liquors, which do conduce very much to the constant health of our inhabitants. Their ordinary course is to breakfast and sup with toast and sider through the whole Lent; which heightens their appetites and creates in them durable strength to labour.

There was a pause, and our friend (he is a man of girth and with a brow bearing all the candor of a life of intense thought) leaned against the mahogany counter.

That is very fine, we said, draining our chalice, and feeling brightness of eye, length of years, and durable strength to labour added to our person. In the meantime (we said) why do you not drink the rich and winy liquor which your vessel contains?

He folded up his clipping and put it away with a sigh.

I always have to read that first, he said, to make the damned stuff palatable. It will be ten years, he said, before the friend who sent me that clipping will have to drink any cider.

7

ONE-NIGHT STANDS

To those looking for an exhilarating vacation let us commend a week of "trouping" on one-night stands with a theatrical company, which mirthful experience has just been ours. We went along in the very lowly capacity of co-author, which placed us somewhat beneath the stage hands as far as dignity was concerned; and we flatter ourself that we have learned our station and observe it with due humility. The first task of the director who stages a play is to let the author know where he gets off. This was accomplished in our case by an argument concerning a speech in the play where one of the characters remarks, "I propose to send a mental message to Eliza." This sounds (we contend) quite a harmless sentiment, but the director insisted that the person speaking, being an Englishman of studious disposition, would not say anything so inaccurate. "He would use much more correct language," said the director. "He ought to say 'I purpose to send.'" We balked mildly at this. "All right," said our mentor. "The trouble with you is you don't know any English. I'll send you a copy of the Century dictionary."

This gentleman carried purism to almost extravagant lengths. He objected to the customary pronunciation of "jew's-harp," insisting that the word should be "juice-harp," and instructing the actor who mentioned this innocent instrument of melody to write it down so in his script. When the dress rehearsal came round, he was surveying the "set" for the first act with considerable complacence. This scenery was intended to represent a very ancient English inn at Stratford-on-Avon, and one of the authors was heard to remark softly that it looked more like a broker's office on Wall Street. But the director was unshaken. "There's an old English inn up at Larchmont," said he, "and this looks a good deal like it, so I guess we're all right."

Let any one who imagines the actor's life is one of bevo and skittles sally along with a new play on its try-out in the one-night circuit. When one sees the delightful humour, fortitude, and high spirits with which the players face their task he gains a new respect for the profession. It is with a sense of shame that the wincing author hears his lines repeated night after night—lines that seem to him to have grown so stale and disreputably stupid, and which the ingenuity of the players contrives to instill with life. With a sense of shame indeed does he reflect that because one day long ago he was struck with a preposterous idea, here are honest folk depending on it to earn daily bread and travelling on a rainy day on a local train on the Central New England Railway; here are 800 people in Saratoga Springs filing into a theatre with naïve expectation on their faces. Amusing things happen faster than he can stay to count them. A fire breaks out in a cigar store a few minutes before theatre time. It is extinguished immediately, but half the town has rushed down to see the excitement. The cigar store is almost next door to the theatre, and the crowd sees the lighted sign and drops in to give the show the once-over, thus giving one a capacity house. Then there are the amusing accidents that happen on the stage, due to the inevitable confusion of one-night stands with long jumps each day, when scenery and props arrive at the theatre barely in time to be set up. In the third act one of the characters has to take his trousers out of a handbag. He opens the bag, but by some error no garments are within. Heavens! has the stage manager mixed up the bags? He has only one hope. The girlish heroine's luggage is also on the stage, and our comedian dashes over and finds his trousers in her bag. This casts a most sinister imputation on the adorable heroine, but our friend (blessings on him) contrives it so delicately that the audience doesn't get wise. Then doors that are supposed to be locked have a habit of swinging open, and the luckless heroine, ready to say furiously to the hero, "Will you unlock the door?" finds herself facing an open doorway and has to invent a line to get herself off the stage.

Going on the road is a very humanizing experience and one gathers a considerable respect for the small towns one visits. They are so brisk, so proud in their local achievements, so prosperous and so full of attractive shop-windows. When one finds in Johnstown, N. Y., for instance, a bookshop with almost as well-assorted a stock as one would see here in Philadelphia; or in Gloversville and Newburgh public libraries that would be a credit to any large city, one realizes the great tide of public intelligence that has risen perceptibly in recent years. At the hotel in Gloversville the proprietress assured us that "an English duke" had just left who told her that he preferred her hotel to the Biltmore in New York. We rather wondered about this English duke, but we looked him up on the register and found that he was Sir H. Urnick of Fownes Brothers, the glove manufacturers, who have a factory in Gloversville. But then, being a glove manufacturer, he may have been kidding her, as the low comedian of our troupe observed. But the local pride of the small town is a genial thing. It may always be noted in the barber shops. The small-town barber knows his

9

customers and when a strange face appears to be shaved on the afternoon when the bills are announcing a play, he puts two and two together. "Are you with that show?" he asks; and being answered in the affirmative (one naturally would not admit that one is merely there in the frugal capacity of co-author, and hopes that he will imagine that such a face might conceivably belong to the low comedian) he proceeds to expound the favourite doctrine that this is a wise burg. "Yes," he says, "folks here are pretty cagy. If your show can get by here you needn't worry about New York. Believe me, if you get a hand here you can go right down to Broadway. I always take in the shows, and I've heard lots of actors say this town is harder to please than any place they ever played."

One gets a new viewpoint on many matters by a week of one-night stands. Theatrical billboards, for instance. We had always thought, in a vague kind of way, that they were a defacement to a town and cluttered up blank spaces in an unseemly way. But when you are trouping, the first thing you do, after registering at the hotel, is to go out and scout round the town yearning for billboards and complaining because there aren't enough of them. You meet another member of the company on the same errand and say, "I don't see much paper out," this being the technical phrase. You both agree that the advance agent must be loafing. Then you set out to see what opposition you are playing against, and emit groans on learning that "The Million Dollar Doll in Paris" is also in town, or "Harry Bulger's Girly Show" will be there the following evening, or Mack Sennett's Bathing Beauties in Person. "That's the kind of stuff they fall for," said the other author mournfully, and you hustle around to the box office to see whether the ticket rack is still full of unsold pasteboard.

At this time of year, when all the metropolitan theatres are crowded and there are some thirty plays cruising round in the offing waiting for a chance to get into New York and praying that some show now there will "flop," one crosses the trail of many other wandering troupes that are battering about from town to town. In remote Johnstown, N. Y., which can only be reached by trolley and where there is no hotel (but a very fine large theatre) one finds that Miss Grace George is to be the next attraction. On the train to Saratoga one rides on the same train with the Million Dollar Doll, and those who have seen her "paper" on the billboards in Newburgh or Poughkeepsie keep an attentive optic open for the lady herself to see how nearly she lives up to her lithographs. And if the passerby should see a lighted window in the hotel glimmering at two in the morning, he will probably aver that there are some of those light-

10

hearted "show people" carousing over a flagon of Virginia Dare. Little does he suspect that long after the tranquil thespians have gone to their well-earned hay, the miserable authors of the trying-out piece may be vigiling together, trying to dope out a new scene for the third act. The saying is not new, but it comes frequently to the lips of the one-night stander—It's a great life if you don't weaken.

THE OWL TRAIN

Across the cold moonlit landscapes, while good folk are at home curling their toes in the warm bottom of the bed, the Owl trains rumble with a gentle drone, neither fast nor slow.

There are several Owl trains with which we have been familiar. One, rather aristocratic of its kind, is the caravan of sleeping cars that leaves New York at midnight and deposits hustling business men of the most aggressive type at the South Station, Boston. After a dissolute progress full of incredible jerks and jolts these pilgrims reach this dampest, darkest, and most Arctic of all terminals about the time the morning codfish begins to warm his bosom on the gridirons of the sacred city. Another, a terrible nocturnal prowler, slips darkly away from Albany about 1 a. m., and rambles disconsolately and with shrill wailings along the West Shore line. Below the grim Palisades of the Hudson it wakes painful echoes. Its first six units, as far as one can see in the dark, are blind express cars, containing milk cans and coffins. We once boarded it at Kingston, and after uneasy slumber across two facing seats found ourself impaled upon Weehawken three hours later. There one treads dubiously upon a ferryboat in the fog and brume of dawn, ungluing eyelids in the bleak dividing pressure of the river breeze.

But the Owl train we propose to celebrate is the vehicle that departs modestly from the crypt of the Pennsylvania Station in New York at half-past midnight and emits blood-shot wanderers at West Philadelphia at 3:16 in the morning. The railroad company, which thinks these problems out with nice care, lulls the passengers into unconsciousness of their woes not only by a gentle and even gait, a progress almost tender in its carefully modulated repression of speed, but also by keeping the cars at such an amazing heat that the victims promptly fade into a swoon. Nowhere will you see a more complete abandonment to the wild postures of fatigue and despair than in the pathetic sprawl of these human forms upon the simmering plush settees. A hot eddy of some varnish-tinctured vapour—certainly not air—rises from under the seats and wraps the traveller in a nightmarish trance. Occasionally he starts wildly from his dream and glares frightfully through the misted pane. It is the custom of the trainmen, who tiptoe softly through the cars, never to disturb their clients by calling out the names of stations. When New Brunswick is reached many think that they have arrived at West

12

Philadelphia, or (worse still) have been carried on to Wilmington. They rush desperately to the bracing chill of the platform to learn where they are. There is a mood of mystery about this Owl of ours. The trainmen take a quaint delight in keeping the actual whereabouts of the caravan a merciful secret.

Oddly assorted people appear on this train. Occasional haughty revellers, in evening dress and opera capes, appear among the humbler voyagers. For a time they stay on their dignity: sit bravely upright and talk with apparent intelligence. Then the drowsy poison of that stifled atmosphere overcomes them, too, and they fall into the weakness of their brethren. They turn over the opposing seat, elevate their nobler shins, and droop languid heads over the ticklish plush chair-back. Strange aliens lie spread over the seats. Nowhere will you see so many faces of curious foreign carving. It seems as though many desperate exiles, who never travel by day, use the Owl for moving obscurely from city to city. This particular train is bound south to Washington, and at least half its tenants are citizens of colour. Even the endless gayety of our dusky brother is not proof against the venomous exhaustion of that boxed-in suffocation. The ladies of his race are comfortably prepared for the hardships of the route. They wrap themselves in huge fur coats and all have sofa cushions to recline on. Even in an all-night session of Congress you will hardly note so complete an abandonment of disillusion, weariness, and cynical despair as is written upon the blank faces all down the aisle. Even the will-power of a George Creel or a Will H. Hays would droop before this three-hour ordeal. Professor Einstein, who talks so delightfully of discarding Time and Space, might here reconsider his theories if he brooded, baking gradually upward, on the hot green plush.

This genial Owl is not supposed to stop at North Philadelphia, but it always does. By this time Philadelphia passengers are awake and gathered in the cold vestibules, panting for escape. Some of them, against the rules of the train, manage to escape on the North Philadelphia platform. The rest, standing huddled over the swaying couplings, find the leisurely transit to West Philadelphia as long as the other segments of the ride put together. Stoically, and beyond the power of words, they lean on one another. At last the train slides down a grade. In the dark and picturesque tunnel of the West Philadelphia station, through thick mists of steam where the glow of the fire box paints the fog a golden rose, they grope and find the ancient stairs. Then they stagger off to seek a lonely car or a night-hawk taxi.

SAFETY PINS

Ligature of infancy, healing engine of emergency, base and mainstay of our civilization—we celebrate the safety pin.

What would we do without safety pins? Is it not odd to think, looking about us on our fellowmen (bearded realtors, ejaculating poets, plump and ruddy policemen, even the cheerful dusky creature who runs the elevator and whistles "Oh, What a Pal Was Mary" as the clock draws near 6 p. m.)—all these were first housed and swaddled and made seemly with a paper of safety pins. How is it that the inventor who first conferred this great gift on the world is not known by name for the admiration and applause of posterity? Was it not the safety pin that made the world safe for infancy?

There will be some, mayhap, to set up the button as rival to the safety pin in service to humanity. But our homage bends toward the former. Not only was it our shield and buckler when we were too puny and impish to help ourselves, but it is also (now we are parent) symbol of many a hard-fought field, where we have campaigned all over the white counterpane of a large bed to establish an urchin in his proper gear, while he kicked and scrambled, witless of our dismay. It is fortunate, pardee, that human memory does not extend backward to the safety pin era—happily the recording carbon sheet of the mind is not inserted on the roller of experience until after the singular humiliations of earliest childhood have passed. Otherwise our first recollection would doubtless be of the grimly flushed large face of a resolute parent, bending hotly downward in effort to make both ends meet while we wambled and waggled in innocent, maddening sport. In those days when life was (as George Herbert puts it) "assorted sorrows, anguish of all sizes," the safety pin was the only thing that raised us above the bandar-log. No wonder the antique schoolmen used to enjoy computing the number of angels that might dance on the point of a pin. But only archangels would be worthy to pirouette on a safety pin, which is indeed mightier than the sword. When Adam delved and Eve did spin, what did they do for a safety pin?

Great is the stride when an infant passes from the safety pin period to the age of buttons. There are three ages of human beings in this matter: (1) Safety pins, (2) Buttons, (3) Studs, or (for females) Hooks and Eyes. Now there is an interim in the life of man when he passes away from safety pins, and, for a season, knows them not—

save as mere convenience in case of breakdown. He thinks of them, in his antic bachelor years, as merely the wrecking train of the sartorial system, a casual conjunction for pyjamas, or an impromptu hoist for small clothes. Ah! with humility and gratitude he greets them again later, seeing them at their true worth, the symbol of integration for the whole social fabric. Women, with their intuitive wisdom, are more subtle in this subject. They never wholly outgrow safety pins, and though they love to ornament them with jewellery, precious metal, and enamels, they are naught but safety pins after all. Some ingenious philosopher could write a full tractate on woman in her relation to pins—hairpins, clothes pins, rolling pins, hatpins.

Only a bachelor, as we have implied, scoffs at pins. Hamlet remarked, after seeing the ghost, and not having any Sir Oliver Lodge handy to reassure him, that he did not value his life at a pin's fee. Pope, we believe, coined the contemptuous phrase, "I care not a pin." The pin has never been done justice in the world of poetry. As one might say, the pin has had no Pindar. Of course there is the old saw about see a pin and pick it up, all the day you'll have good luck. This couplet, barbarous as it is in its false rhyme, points (as Mother Goose generally does) to a profound truth. When you see a pin, you must pick it up. In other words, it is on the floor, where pins generally are. Their instinctive affinity for terra firma makes one wonder why they, rather than the apple, did not suggest the law of gravitation to someone long before Newton.

Incidentally, of course, the reason why Adam and Eve were forbidden to pick the apple was that it was supposed to stay on the tree until it fell, and Adam would then have had the credit of spotting the principle of gravitation.

Much more might be said about pins, touching upon their curious capacity for disappearing, superstitions concerning them, usefulness of hatpins or hairpins as pipe-cleaners, usefulness of pins to schoolboys, both when bent for fishing and when filed to an extra point for use on the boy in the seat in front (honouring him in the breech, as Hamlet would have said) and their curious habits of turning up in unexpected places, undoubtedly caught by pins in their long association with the lovelier sex. But of these useful hyphens of raiment we will merely conclude by saying that those interested in the pin industry will probably emigrate to England, for we learn from the Encyclopædia Britannica that in that happy island pins are cleaned by being boiled in weak beer. Let it not be forgotten, however, that of all kinds, the safety is the King Pin.

15

CONFESSIONS OF A "COLYUMIST"

I can not imagine any pleasant job so full of pangs, or any painful job so full of pleasures, as the task of conducting a newspaper column.

The colyumist, when he begins his job, is disheartened because nobody notices it. He soon outgrows this, and is disheartened because too many people notice it, and he imagines that all see the paltriness of it as plainly as he does. There is nothing so amazing to him as to find that any one really enjoys his "stuff." Poor soul, he remembers how he groaned over it at his desk. He remembers the hours he sat with lack-lustre eye and addled brain, brooding at the sluttish typewriter. He remembers the flush of shame that tingled him as he walked sadly homeward, thinking of some atrocious inanity he had sent upstairs to the composing-room. It is a job that engenders a healthy humility.

I had always wanted to have a try at writing a column. Heaven help me, I think I had an idea that I was born for the job. I may as well be candid. There was a time when I seriously thought of inserting the following ad in a Philadelphia newspaper. I find a memorandum of it in my scrap-book:

> Humorist: Young and untamed, lineal descendent of Eugene Field, Frank Stockton, and François Rabelais, desires to run a column in a Philadelphia newspaper. A guaranteed circulation-getter.

> Said Humorist can also supply excellent veins of philosophy, poetry, satire, uplift, glad material and indiscriminate musings. Remarkable opportunity for any newspaper desiring a really unusual editorial feature. Address Humorist, etc.

So besotted was I, I would have paid to have this printed if I had not been counselled by an older and wiser head.

I instance this to show that the colyumist is likely to begin his job with the conception that it is to be a perpetual uproar of mirth and high spirits. This lasts about a week. He then learns, in secret, to take it rather seriously. He has to deal with the most elusive and grotesque material he knows—his own mind; and the unhappy

16

creature, everlastingly probing himself in the hope of discovering what is so rare in minds (a thought), is likely to end in a ferment of bitterness. The happiest times in life are when one can just live along and enjoy things as they happen. If you have to be endlessly speculating, watching, and making mental notes, your brain-gears soon get a hot box. The original of all paragraphers—Ecclesiastes— came very near ending as a complete cynic; though in what F. P. A. would call his "lastline," he managed to wriggle into a more hopeful mood.

The first valuable discovery that the colyumist is likely to make is that all minds are very much the same. The doctors tell us that all patent medicines are built on a stock formula—a sedative, a purge, and a bitter. If you are to make steady column-topers out of your readers, your daily dose must, as far as possible, average up to that same prescription. If you employ the purge all the time, or the sedative, or the acid, your clients will soon ask for something with another label.

Don Marquis once wrote an admirable little poem called "A Colyumist's Prayer." Mr. Marquis, who is the king of all colyumists, realizes that there is what one may call a religious side in colyumizing. It is hard to get the colyumist to admit this, for he fears spoofing worse than the devil; but it is eminently true. If I were the owner of a newspaper, I think I would have painted up on the wall of the local room the following words from Isaiah, the best of all watchwords for all who write:

> Woe unto them that call evil good, and good evil; that put darkness for light, and light for darkness; that put bitter for sweet, and sweet for bitter!

The most painful privilege of the colyumist's job is the number of people who drop in to see him, usually when he is imprecating his way toward the hour of going to press. This is all a part of the great and salutary human instinct against work. When people see a man toiling, they have an irresistible impulse to crowd round and stop him. They seem to imagine that he has been put there on purpose to help them solve their problems, to find a job for their friend from Harrisburg, or to tell them how to find a publisher for their poems. Unhappily, their victim being merely human, is likely to grow a bit snappish under infliction. Yet now and then he gets a glimpse into a human vexation so sincere, so honest, and so moving that he turns away from the typewriter with a sigh. He wonders how one dare approach the chronicling of this muddled panorama with anything

17

but humility and despair. Frank Harris once said of Oscar Wilde: "If England insists on treating her criminals like this, she doesn't deserve to have any." Similarly, if the public insists on bringing its woes to its colyumists, it doesn't deserve to have any colyumists. Then the battered jester turns again to his machine and ticks off something like this:

> We have heard of ladies who have been tempted beyond their strength. We have also seen some who have been strengthened beyond their temptation.

Of course there are good days, too. (This is not one of them.) Days when the whole course of the news seems planned for the benefit of the chaffish and irreverent commentator. When Governor Hobby of Texas issues a call for the state cavalry. When one of your clients drops in, in the goodness of his heart, to give you his own definition of a pessimist—a pessimist, he says, is a man who wears both belt and suspenders. When a big jewellery firm in the city puts out a large ad—

> Bailey, Banks & Biddle Company Watches for Women Of Superior Design and Perfection of Movement

all that one needs to do to that is to write over it the caption

SO DO WE ALL

and pass on to the next paragraph.

The more a colyumist is out on the streets, making himself the reporter of the moods and oddities of men, the better his stuff will be. It seems to me that his job ought to be good training for a novelist, as it teaches him a habit of human sensitiveness. He becomes filled with an extraordinary curiosity about the motives and purposes of the people he sees. The other afternoon I was very much struck by the unconscious pathos of a little, gentle-eyed old man who was standing on Chestnut Street studying a pocket notebook. His umbrella leaned against a shop-window, on the sill of which he had laid a carefully rolled-up newspaper. By his feet was a neat leather brief-case, plumply filled with contents not discernible. There he stood (a sort of unsuccessful Cyrus Curtis), very diminutive, his gray hair rather long abaft his neck, his yellowish straw hat (with curly brim) tilted backward as though in perplexity, his timid and absorbed blue eyes poring over his memorandum-book which was full of pencilled notes. He had a slightly unkempt,

18

brief beard and whiskers, his cheek-bones pinkish, his linen a little frayed. There was something strangely pathetic about him, and I would have given much to have been able to speak to him. I halted at a window farther down the street and studied him; then returned to pass him again, and watched him patiently. He stood quite absorbed, and was still there when I went on.

That is just one of the thousands of vivid little pictures one sees on the city streets day by day. To catch some hint of the meaning of all this, to present a few scrawled notes of the amazing interest and colour of the city's life, this is the colyumist's task as I see it. It is a task not a whit less worthy, less painful, or less baffling than that of the most conscientious novelist. And it is carried on in surroundings of extraordinary stimulation and difficulty. It is heart-racking to struggle day by day, amid incessant interruption and melee, to snatch out of the hurly-burly some shreds of humour or pathos or (dare one say?) beauty, and phrase them intelligibly.

But it is fun. One never buys a package of tobacco, crosses a city square, enters a trolley-car or studies a shop-window without trying, in a baffled, hopeless way, to peer through the frontage of the experience, to find some glimmer of the thoughts, emotions, and meanings behind. And in the long run such a habit of inquiry must bear fruit in understanding and sympathy. Joseph Conrad (who seems, by the way, to be more read by newspaper men than any other writer) put very nobly the pinnacle of all scribblers' dreams when he said that human affairs deserve the tribute of "a sigh which is not a sob, a smile which is not a grin."

So much, with apology, for the ideals of the colyumist, if he be permitted to speak truth without fear of mockery. Of course in the actual process and travail of his job you will find him far different. You may know him by a sunken, brooding eye; clothing marred by much tobacco, and a chafed and tetchy humour toward the hour of five p. m. Having bitterly schooled himself to see men as paragraphs walking, he finds that his most august musings have a habit of stewing themselves down to some ferocious or jocular three-line comment. He may yearn desperately to compose a really thrilling poem that will speak his passionate soul; to churn up from the typewriter some lyric that will rock with blue seas and frantic hearts; he finds himself allaying the frenzy with some jovial sneer at Henry Ford or a yell about the High Cost of Living. Poor soul, he is like one condemned to harangue the vast, idiotic world through a keyhole, whence his anguish issues thin and faint. Yet who will say that all his labour is wholly vain? Perhaps some day the government will crown a Colyumist Laureate, some majestic sage with ancient patient blue eyes and a snowy beard nobly stained with nicotine, whose utterances will be heeded with shuddering respect. All minor colyumists will wear robes and sandals; they will be an order of scoffing friars; people will run to them on crowded streets to lay before them the sorrows and absurdities of men. And in that day

> The meanest paragraph that blows will give
> Thoughts that do often lie too deep for sneers.

20

MOVING

Man, we suspect, is the only animal capable of persuading himself that his hardships are medicine to the soul, of flattering himself into a conviction that some mortal spasm was a fortifying discipline.

Having just moved our household goods for the fourth time in four years, we now find ourself in the singular state of trying to believe that the horrors of the event have added to our supply of spiritual resignation. Well, let us see.

The brutal task of taking one's home on trek is (we can argue) a stirring tonic, a kind of private rehearsal of the Last Judgment, when the sheep shall be divided from the shoats. What could be a more convincing reminder of the instability of man's affairs than the harrowing upheaval of our cherished properties? Those dark angels, the moving men, how heartless they seem in their brisk and resolute dispassion—yet how exactly they prefigure the implacable sternness of the ultimate shepherds. A strange life is theirs, taking them day after day into the bosom of homes prostrated by the emigrating throe. Does this matter-of-fact bearing conceal an infinite tenderness, a pity that dare not show itself for fear of unmanly collapse? Are they secretly broken by the sight of the desolate nursery, the dismantled crib, the forgotten clockwork monkey lying in a corner of the cupboard where the helpless Urchin laid it with care before he and his smaller sister were deported, to be out of the way in the final storm? Does the o'ermastering pathos of a modest household turned inside out, its tender vitals displayed to the passing world, wring their breasts? Stoic men, if so, they well conceal their pangs.

They have one hopelessly at a disadvantage. In the interval that always elapses before the arrival of the second van, there is a little social chat and utterance of reminiscences. There is a lively snapping of matchheads on thumbnails, and seated at ease in the débris of the dismantled living room our friends will tell of the splendour of some households they have moved before. The thirty-eight barrels of gilt porcelain, the twenty cases of oil paintings, the satin-wood grand piano that their spines twinge to recall. Once our furnitures were moved by a crew of lusty athletes who had previously done the same for Mr. Ivy Lee, and while we sat in shamed silence we heard the tale of Mr. Lee's noble possessions. Of what avail would it have been for us to protest that we love our stuff as much as Mr. Lee did his? No, we had a horrid impulse to cry apology, and beg them to hurl the things into the van anyhow, just to end the agony.

This interval of social chat being prolonged by the blizzard, the talk is likely to take a more ominous turn. We are told how, only last week, a sister van was hit by a train at a crossing and carried a hundred yards on the engine pilot. Two of the men were killed, though one of these lived from eleven o'clock Saturday morning until eleven o'clock Monday night. How, after hearing this, can one ask what happened to the furniture, even if one is indecent enough to think of it? Then one learns of another of the fleet, stalled in a drift on the way to Harrisburg, and hasn't been heard from for forty-eight hours. Sitting in subdued silence, one remembers something about "moving accidents by flood and field," and thanks fortune that these pitiful oddments are only going to a storage warehouse, not to be transported thence until the kindly season of spring.

But packing for storage instead of for moving implies subtler and more painful anguishes. Here indeed we have a tonic for the soul, for election must be made among one's belongings: which are to be stored, and which to accompany? Take the subject of books for instance. Horrid hesitation: can we subsist for four or five months on nothing but the "Oxford Book of English Verse" and Boswell's Johnson? Suppose we want to look up a quotation, in those late hours of the night when all really worthwhile reading is done? Our memory is knitted with a wide mesh. Suppose we want to be sure just what it was that Shakespeare said happened to him in his "sessions of sweet silent thought," what are we going to do? We will have to fall back on the customary recourse of the minor poet—if you can't remember one of Shakespeare's sonnets, at least you can write one of your own instead. Speaking of literature, it is a curious thing that the essayists have so neglected this topic of moving. It would be pleasant to know how the good and the great have faced this peculiarly terrible crisis of domestic affairs. When the Bard himself moved back to Stratford after his years in London, what did he think about it? How did he get all his papers packed up, and did he, in mere weariness, destroy the half-done manuscripts of plays? Charles Lamb moved round London a good deal; did he never write of his experience? We like to think of Emerson: did he ever move, and if so, how did he behave when the fatal day came? Did he sit on a packing case and utter sepulchral aphorisms? Think of Lord Bacon and how he would have crystallized the matter in a phrase.

22

Of course in bachelor days moving may be a huge lark, a humorous escapade. We remember some high-spirited young men, three of them, who were moving their chattels from rooms on Twenty-first Street to a flat on Irving Place. Frugality was their necessary watchword, and they hired a pushcart in which to transport the dunnage. It was necessary to do this on Sunday, and one of the trio, more sensitive than the others, begged that they should rise and accomplish the public shame early in the morning, before the streets were alive. In particular, he begged, let the route be chosen to avoid a certain club on Gramercy Park where he had many friends, and where he was loath to be seen pushing his humble intimacies. The others, scenting sport, and brazenly hardy of spirit, contrived to delay the start on one pretext or another until the middle of the forenoon. Then, by main force, ignoring his bitter protest, they impelled the staggering vehicle, grossly overloaded, past the very door of the club my friend had wished to avoid. Here, by malicious inspiration, they tilted the wain to one side and strewed the paving with their property. They skipped nimbly round the corner, and with highly satisfactory laughter watched their blushing partner labouring dismally to collect the fragments. Some of his friends issuing from the club lent a hand, and the joy of the conspirators was complete.

But to the family man, moving is no such airy picnic. Sadly he goes through the last dismal rites and sees the modest fragments of his dominion hustled toward the cold sepulture of a motor van. Before the toughened bearing of the hirelings he doubts what manner to assume. Shall he stand at the front door and exhort them to particular care with each sentimental item, crying "Be careful with that little chair; that's the one the Urchin uses when he eats his evening prunes!" Or shall he adopt a gruesome sarcasm, hoping to awe them by conveying the impression that even if the whole van should be splintered in collision, he can get more at the nearest department store? Whatever policy he adopts, they will not be much impressed. For, when we handed our gratuity, not an ungenerous one, to the driver, asking him to divide it among the gang, we were startled to hear them burst into loud screams of mirth. We asked, grimly, the cause. It appeared that during the work one of our friends, apparently despairing of any pourboire appropriate to his own conceptions of reward, had sold his share of the tip to the driver for fifteen cents. We are not going to say how much he lost by so doing. But this gamble put the driver in such a good humour that we believe he will keep away from railroad crossings.

23

SURF FISHING

All day long you see them stand thigh-deep in the surf, fishing. Up on the beach each one has a large basket containing clams for bait, extra hooks and leaders, a little can of oil for the reel, and any particular doo-dads dear to the heart of the individual fisherman. And an old newspaper, all ready to protect the anticipated catch from the rays of the sun.

Some of them wear bathing suits; others rubber hip-boots, or simply old clothes that won't mind getting wet. If they are very full of swank they will have a leather belt with a socket to hold the butt of the rod. Every now and then you will see them pacing backward up the beach, reeling in the line. They will mutter something about a big strike that time, and he got away with the bait. With zealous care they spear some more clam on the hook, twisting it over and over the barb so as to be firmly impaled. Then, with careful precision, they fling the line with its heavy pyramid sinker far out beyond the line of breakers.

There they stand. What do they think about, one wonders? But what does any one think about when fishing? That is one of the happy pastimes that don't require much thinking. The long ridges of surf crumble about their knees and the sun and keen vital air lull them into a cheerful drowse of the faculties. Do they speculate on the never-ending fascination of the leaning walls of water, the rhythmical melody of the rasp and hiss of the water? Do they watch that indescribable beauty of the breaking wave, a sight as old as humankind and yet never so described that one who has not seen it could picture it?

The wave gathers height and speed as it moves toward the sand. It seems to pull itself together for the last plunge. The first wave that ever rolled up to a beach probably didn't break. It just slid. It was only the second wave that broke—curled over in that curious way. For our theory—which may be entirely wrong—is that the breaking is due to the undertow of previous waves. After a wave sprawls up on the beach, it runs swiftly back. This receding undercurrent—you can feel it very strongly if you are swimming just in front of a large wave about to break—digs in beneath the advancing hill of water. It cuts away the foundations of that hill, which naturally topples over at the crest.

The wave of water leans and hangs for a delaying instant. The actual cascade may begin at one end and run along the length of the ridge; it may begin at both ends and twirl inward, meeting in the middle; it may (but very rarely) begin in the middle and work outward. As the billow is at its height, before it combs over, the fisherman sees the sunlight gleaming through it—an ecstasy of perfect lucid green, with the glimmer of yellow sand behind. Then, for a brief moment—so brief that the details can never be memorized—he sees a clear crystal screen of water falling forward. Another instant, and it is all a boil of snowy suds seething about his legs. He may watch it a thousand times, a million times; it will never be old, never wholly familiar. Colour varies from hour to hour, from day to day. Sometimes blue or violet, sometimes green-olive or gray. The backwash tugs at his boots, hollowing out little channels under his feet. The sun wraps him round like a mantle; the salt crusts and thickens in his hair. And then, when he has forgotten everything save the rhythm of the falling waves, there comes a sudden tug——

He reels in, and a few curious bathers stand still in the surf to see what he has got. They are inclined to be scornful. It is such a little fish! One would think that such a vast body of water would be ashamed to yield only so small a prize. Never mind. He has compensations they wot not of. Moreover—although he would hardly admit it himself—the fishing business is only a pretext. How else could a grown man with grizzled hair have an excuse to stand all day paddling in the surf?

"IDOLATRY"

Once in a while, when the name of R. L. S. is mentioned in conversation, someone says to us: "Ah well, you're one of the Stevenson idolators, aren't you?" And this is said with a curious air of cynical superiority, as of one who has experienced all these things and is superbly tolerant of the shallow mind that can still admire Tusitala. His work (such people will generally tell you) was brilliant but "artificial" ... and for the true certificated milk of the word one must come along to such modern giants as Dreiser and Hergesheimer and Cabell. For these artists, each in his due place, we have only the most genial respect. But when the passion of our youth is impugned as "idolatry" we feel in our spirit an intense weariness. We feel the pacifism of the wise and secretive mind that remains tacit when its most perfect inward certainties are assailed. One does not argue, for there are certain things not arguable. One shrugs. After all, what human gesture more eloquent (or more satisfying to the performer) than the shrug?

There is a little village on the skirts of the Forest of Fontainebleau (heavenly region of springtime and romance!) where the crystal-green eddies of the Loing slip under an old gray bridge with sharp angled piers of stone. Near the bridge is a quiet little inn, one of the many happy places in that country long frequented by artists for painting and "villégiature." Behind the inn is a garden beside the river-bank. The salle à manger, as in so many of those inns at Barbizon, Moret, and the other Fontainebleau villages, is panelled and frescoed with humorous and high-spirited impromptus done by visiting painters.

In the summer of 1876 an anxious rumour passed among the artist colonies. It was said that an American lady and her two children had arrived at Grez, and the young bohemians who regarded this region as their own sacred retreat were startled and alarmed. Were their chosen haunts to be invaded by tourists—and tourists of the disturbing sex? Among three happy irresponsibles this humorous anxiety was particularly acute. One of the trio was sent over to Grez as a scout, to spy out the situation and report. The emissary went, and failed to return. A second explorer was dispatched to study the problem. He, too, was swallowed up in silence. The third, impatiently waiting tidings from his faithless friends, set out to make an end of this mystery. He reached the inn at dusk: it was a gentle summer evening; the windows were open to the tender air; lamps were lit within, and a merry party sat at dinner. Through the open window the suspicious venturer saw the recreant ambassadors, gay with laughter. And there, sitting in the lamplight, was the American lady—a slender, thoughtful enchantress with eyes as dark and glowing as the wine. Thus it was that Robert Louis Stevenson first saw Fanny Osbourne.

A few days later Mrs. Osbourne's eighteen-year-old daughter Isobel wrote in a letter: "There is a young Scotchman here, a Mr. Stevenson. He is such a nice-looking ugly man, and I would rather listen to him talk than read the most interesting book.... Mama is ever so much better and is getting prettier every day."

"The Life of Mrs. Robert Louis Stevenson," written by her sister Mrs. Sanchez (the mother of "little Louis Sanchez on the beach at Monterey" remembered by lovers of "A Child's Garden of Verses") is a book that none of the so-called idolaters will want to overlook. The romantic excitements of R. L. S.'s youth were tame indeed compared to those of Fanny Van de Grift. R. L. S. had been thrilled enough by a few nights spent in the dark with the docile ass of the Cevennes; but here was one, sprung from sober Philadelphia blood, born in Indianapolis and baptized by Henry Ward Beecher, who had pioneered across the fabled Isthmus, lived in the roaring mining camps of Nevada, worked for a dressmaker in Frisco, and venturously taken her young children to Belgium and France to study art. She had been married at seventeen, had already once thought herself to be a widow in fact by the temporary disappearance of her first husband; and was now, after enduring repeated infidelities, prepared to make herself a widow in law. Daring horse woman, a good shot, a supreme cook, artist, writer, and a very Gene Stratton Porter among flowers, fearless, beautiful, and of unique charm—where could another woman have been found so marvellously gifted to be the wife of a romancer? It seems odd that Philadelphia and Edinburgh, the two most conservatively minded cities of the Anglo-Saxon earth, should have combined to produce this, the most radiant pair of adventurers in our recent annals.

The reading of this delightful book has taken us back into the very pang and felicity of our first great passion—our idolatry, if you will—which we are proud here and now to re-avow. When was there ever a happier or more wholesome worship for a boy than the Stevenson mania on which so many of this generation grew up? We were the

27

luckier in that our zeal was shared in all its gusto and particularity by a lean, long-legged, sallow-faced, brown-eyed eccentric (himself incredibly Stevensonian in appearance) with whom we lay afield in our later teens, reading R. L. S. aloud by the banks of a small stream which we vowed should become famous in the world of letters. And so it has, though not by our efforts, which was what we had designed; for at the crystal headwater of that same creek was penned "The Amenities of Book Collecting," that enchanting volume of bookish essays which has swelled the correspondence of a Philadelphia business man to insane proportions, and even brought him offers from three newspapers to conduct a book page. It seems appropriate to the present chronicler that in a quiet library overlooking the clear fount and origin of dear Darby Creek there are several of the most cherished association volumes of R. L. S.—we think particularly of the "Child's Garden of Verses" which he gave to Cummy, and the manuscript of little "Smoutie's" very first book, the "History of Moses."

Was there ever a more joyous covenant of affection than that of Mifflin McGill and ourself in our boyish madness for Tusitala? It is a happy circumstance, we say, for a youth, before the multiplying responsibilities of maturity press upon him, to pour out his enthusiasm in an obsession such as that; and when this passion can be shared and doubled and knitted in partnership with an equally freakish, insane, and innocent idiot (such as our generously mad friend Mifflin) admirable adventures are sure to follow. The quest begun on Darby Creek took us later on an all-summer progress among places in England and Scotland hallowed to us by association with R. L. S. Never, in any young lives past or to come, could there be an instant of purer excitement and glory than when, after bicycling hotly all day with the blue outline of Arthur's Seat apparently always receding before us, we trundled grimly into Auld Reekie and set out for the old Stevenson home at 17 Heriot Row, halting only to bestow our pneumatic steeds in the nearest and humblest available hostelry. There (for we found the house empty and "To Let") we sat on the doorstep evening by evening, smoking in the long northern twilight and spinning our youthful dreams. This lust for hunting out our favourite author's footsteps even led one of the pair to a place perhaps never visited by any other Stevensonian pilgrim—old Cockfield Rectory, in Suffolk, where Mrs. Sitwell and Sidney Colvin first met the bright-eyed Scotch boy in 1873. The tracker of footprints remembers how kind were the then occupants of the old rectory, and how, in a daze of awe, he trod the green and tranquil lawn and hastened to visit a cottage near by

28

where there was an ancient rustic who had been coachman at the rectory when R. L. S. stayed there, fabled to retain some pithy recollection. Alas, the Suffolk ancient, eager enough to share tobacco and speech, would only mull over his memories of a previous rector, describing how it had fallen to him to prepare the good man for burial; how he smiled in death and his cheeks were as rosy as a babe's.

It would take many pages to narrate all the bypaths and happy excursions trod by these simple youths in their quest of the immortal Louis. The memories come bustling, and one knows not where to stop. The supreme adventure, for one of the pair, lay in the kindness of Sir Sidney Colvin. To this prince of gentlemen and scholars one of these lads wrote, sending his letter (with subtle cunning) from a village in Suffolk only a few miles from Sir Sidney's boyhood home. He calculated that this might arouse the interest of Sir Sidney, whom he knew to be cruelly badgered with letters from enthusiasts; and fortune turned in his favour, granting him numerous ecstatic visits to Sir Sidney and Lady Colvin and much unwarranted generosity. But, since our mind has been turned in this direction by Mrs. Sanchez's book, it might be appropriate to add that one of the most thrilling moments in the crusade was a season of April days spent beside the green and stripling Loing, in the forest of Fontainebleau region, visiting those lovely French villages where R. L. S. roamed as a young man, crowned by an afternoon at Grez. One remembers the old gray bridge across the eddying water, and the door of the inn where the young pilgrim lingered, trying to visualize scenes of thirty-five years before.

It is not mere idolatry when the hearts of the young are haunted by such spells. There was some real divinity behind the enchantment, some marvellous essence that made all roads Tusitala trod the Road of Loving Hearts. In these matters we would trust the simple Samoans to come nearer the truth than our cynic friend in Greenwich Village. The magic of that great name abides unimpaired.

THE FIRST COMMENCEMENT ADDRESS

(Delivered to Cain and Abel, the first graduating class of the
Garden of Eden Normal School.)

My young friends—It is a privilege to be permitted to address you this morning, for I am convinced that never in the world's history did the age beckon with so eager a gesture to the young men on the threshold of active life. Never indeed in the past, and certainly never in the future, was there or will there be a time more deeply fraught with significance. And as I gaze upon your keen faces it seems almost as though the world had amassed all the problems that now confront us merely in order to give you tasks worthy of your prowess.

The world, I think I may safely say, is smaller now than ever before. The recent invention of young women, something quite new in the way of a social problem, has introduced a hitherto undreamed-of complexity into human affairs. The extreme rapidity with which ideas and thoughts now circulate, due to the new invention of speech, makes it probable that what is said in Eden to-day will be known in the land of Nod within a year. The greatest need is plainly for big-visioned and purposeful men, efficient men, men with forward-looking minds. I hope you will pattern after your admirable father in this respect; he truly was a forward-looking man, for he had nothing to look back on.

You are aware, however, that your father has had serious problems to deal with, and it is well that you should consider those problems in the light of the experiences you are about to face. One of his most perplexing difficulties would never have come upon him if he had not fallen into a deep sleep. I counsel you, therefore, be wary not to overslumber. The prizes of life always come to those who press resolutely on, undaunted by fatigue and discouragement. Another of your father's failings was probably due to the fact that he was never a small boy and thus had no chance to work the deviltry out of his system. You yourselves have been abundantly blessed in this regard. I think I may say that here, in our Normal Academy, you have had an almost ideal playground to work off those boyish high spirits, to perpetrate those mischievous pranks that the world expects of its young. Remember that you are now going out into the mature work of life, where you will encounter serious problems.

As you wend your way from these accustomed shades into the full glare of public life you will do so, I hope, with the consciousness that the eyes of the world are upon you. The sphere of activity in which you may find yourselves called upon to perform may be restricted, but you will remember that not failure but low aim is base. You will hold a just balance between the conflicting tendencies of radicalism and conservatism. You will endeavour to secure for labour its due share in the profits of labour. You will not be forgetful that all government depends in the last resort on the consent of the governed. These catch words in the full flush of your youth you may be inclined to dismiss as truisms, but I assure you that 10,000 years from now men will be uttering them with the same air of discovery.

It is my great pleasure to confer upon you both the degree of bachelor of arts and to pray that you may never bring discredit upon your alma mater.

THE DOWNFALL OF GEORGE SNIPE

George Snipe was an ardent book-lover, and sat in the smoking car in a state of suspended ecstasy. He had been invited out to Mandrake Park to visit the library of Mr. Genial Girth, the well-known collector of rare autographed books. Devoted amateur of literature as he was, George's humble career rarely brought him into contact with bookish treasures, and a tremulous excitement swam through his brain as he thought of the glories he was about to see. In his devout meditation the train carried him a station beyond his alighting place, and he ran frantically back through the well-groomed suburban countryside in order to reach Mr. Girth's home on time.

They went through the library together. Mr. Girth displayed all his fascinating prizes with generous good nature, and George grew excited. The palms of his hands were clammy with agitation. All round the room, encased in scarlet slip-covers of tooled morocco, on fireproof shelves, were the priceless booty of the collector. Here was Charles Lamb's "Essays of Elia," inscribed by the author to the woman he loved. Here was a copy of "Paradise Lost," signed by John Milton. Here was a "Hamlet" given by Shakespeare to Bacon with the inscription, "Dear Frank, don't you wish you could have written something like this?" Here was the unpublished manuscript of a story by Robert Louis Stevenson. Here was a note written by Doctor Johnson to the landlord of the Cheshire Cheese, refusing to pay a bill and accusing the tavern-keeper of profiteering. Here were volumes autographed by Goldsmith, Keats, Shelley, Poe, Byron, DeFoe, Swift, Dickens, Thackeray, and all the other great figures of modern literature.

Poor George's agitation became painful. His head buzzed as he surveyed the faded signatures of all these men who had become the living figures of his day-dreams. His eye rolled wildly in its orbit. Just then Mr. Girth was called out of the room, and left George alone among the treasures.

Just at what instant the mania seized him we shall never know. There were a pen and an inkpot on the table, and the frenzied lover of books dipped the quill deep in the dark blue fluid. He ran eagerly to the shelves. The first volume he saw was a copy of "Lorna Doone." In it he wrote "Affectionately yours, R. D. Blackmore."

32

Then came Longfellow's poems. He scrawled "With deep esteem, Henry W. Longfellow" on the flyleaf. Then three volumes of Macaulay's "History of England." In the first he jotted "I have always wanted you to have these admirable books, T. B. M." In "The Mill on the Floss" he wrote "This comes to you still warm from the press, George Eliot." The next book happened to be a copy of Edgar Guest's poems. In this he inscribed "You are the host I love the best, This is my boast, Yours, Edgar Guest." In a copy of Browning's Poems he wrote "To my dear and only wife, Elizabeth, from her devoted Robert." In a pamphlet reprint of the Gettysburg Speech he penned "This is straight stuff, A. Lincoln." But perhaps his most triumphant exploit was signing a copy of the Rubaiyat thus: "This book is given to the Anti-Saloon League of Naishapur by that thorn in their side, O. Khayyam."

By the time the ambulance reached Mr. Girth's home George was completely beyond control. He was taken away screaming because he had not had a chance to autograph a copy of the "Songs of Solomon."

MEDITATIONS OF A BOOKSELLER

(Roger Mifflin loquitur)

I had a pleasant adventure to-day. A free verse poet came in to see me, wanted me to buy some copies of "The Pagan Anthology." I looked over the book, to which he himself had contributed some pieces. I advised him to read Tennyson. I wish you could have seen his face.

If you want to see a really good anthology (I said) have a look at Pearsall Smith's "Treasury of English Prose," just out. The only thing that surprises me is that Mr. Smith didn't include some free verse in it. The best thing about free verse is that it is often awfully good prose.

It's a superb clear night: a milky pallor washed in the blue: a white moon overhead: stars rare but brilliant, one in the south twinkles and flutters like a tiny flower stirred by faint air. The wind is "a cordial of incredible virtue" (Emerson)—sharp and chill, but with a milder tincture. To-day, though brisk and snell on the streets, the sunshine had a lively vigour, a generous quality, a promissory note of the equinox. I felt it from first rising this morning—the old demiurge at work! As I sat in the bathtub (when a man is fifty he may be pardoned for taking a warm bath on winter mornings) my mind fell upon the desire of wandering: it occurred to me that a spread of legs in the vital air would be richly repaid. The windows called me: as soon as shirt and trousers were on, I was at the sill peering out over Gissing Street. Later, even through closed panes, the chink of milk bottles on the pavement below seemed to rise with a clearer, merrier note. Setting out for some tobacco about 8:30, I stopped to study the ice-man's great blocks of silvery translucence, lying along the curb by a big apartment house. "Artificial" ice, I suppose: it was interesting to see, in the meridian of each cake, a kind of silvery fracture or membrane, with the grain of air-bubbles tending outward therefrom—showing, no doubt, if one knew the mechanics of refrigeration, just how the freezing proceeded. Even in so humble a thing as a block of ice are these harmonic and lovely patterns, the seal of Nature's craft, inscrutable, inimitable. I might have made a point of this in talking to that free verse poet. I'm glad I didn't, however: he would have had some tedious reply, convincing to himself. That's the trouble with replies: they are always

34

convincing to the replier. As a friend of mine used to say, one good taciturn deserves another.

I was thinking, as I took a parcel of laundry up to the Chinaman on McFee Street just now, it would be interesting to write a book dealing solely, candidly, exactly, and fully with the events, emotions, and thoughts of just one day in a man's life. If one could do that, in a way to carry conviction, assent, and reality, to convey to the reader's senses a recognition of genuine actual human being, one might claim to be a true artist.

I have found an admirable book for reading in bed—this little anthology of prose, collected by Pearsall Smith. He knows what good prose is, having written some of the daintiest bits of our time in his "Trivia," a book with which I occasionally delight a truly discerning customer. What a fascination there is in good prose— "the cool element of prose" as Milton calls it—a sort of fluid happiness of the mind, unshaken by the violent pangs of great poetry. I am not subtle enough to describe it, but in the steadily cumulating satisfaction of first-class prose there seems to be something that speaks direct to the brain, unmarred by the claims of the senses, the emotions. I meditate much, ignorantly and fumblingly, on the modes and purposes of writing. It is so simple— "Fool!" said my Muse to me, "look in thy heart and write!"—all that is needful is to tell what happens; and yet how hard it is to summon up that necessary candor. Every time I read great work I see the confirmation of what I grope for. How vivid, straight, and cleanly it seems when done: merely the outward utterance of "what the mind at home, in the spacious circuits of her musing, hath liberty to propose to herself." Let a man's mind depart from his audience; let him have no concern whether to shock or to please. Let him carry no consideration save to utter, with unsparing fidelity, what passes in his own spirit. One can trust the brain to do its part. All that is needed is honourable frankness: not to be ashamed to open our hearts, to speak our privy weakness, our inward exulting. Then the pain and perplexity, or the childish satisfactions, of our daily life are the true material of the writer's art, and that which is sown in weakness may be raised in power. Curious indeed that in this life, brief and precariously enjoyed, men should so set their hearts on building a permanence in words: something to stand, in the lovely stability of ink and leaden types, as our speech out of silence to those who follow on. Indefensible absurdity, and yet the secret and impassioned dream of those who write!

I was about to say that, for the writing of anything truly durable, the first requisite is plenty of silence. Then I recall Dr. Johnson's preface to his Dictionary—"written not in the soft obscurities of retirement, or under the shelter of academic bowers, but amid inconvenience and distraction, in sickness and in sorrow."

IF BUYING A MEAL WERE LIKE BUYING A HOUSE

This Indenture

between A. B., an innkeeper, organized and existing under the laws of good cooking, party of the first part, and C. D., party of the second part, witnesseth:

That the said party of the first part, for and in consideration of the sum of $1.50, lawful money of the United States, paid by the said party of the second part, does hereby grant and release unto the said C. D., and his heirs, administrators, and assigns forever,

All that certain group, parcels, or allotments of food, viands, or victuals, situate or to be spread, served, and garnished upon the premises of said A. B., shown and known and commonly designed as one square meal, table d'hôte, together with the drinking water, napkin, ash tray, finger-bowl and hat-and-coat-hanging privileges or easements appurtenant thereto,

And Together With the rights, privileges, and opportunities (as an easement additionally appurtenant to the meal above nominated) to partake, eat, enjoy, and be nourished upon said victuals, and to call for extra pats, parcels, or portions of butter.

Subject to the following restrictions, to wit: That neither the party of the second part, nor his heirs, executors, or assigns, will feast immoderately upon onions, to the confusion of his neighbours; nor will the said C. D. or his guests smoke any form of tobacco other than cigars and cigarettes, the instrument commonly known as a pipe being offensive to the head waiter (a man of delicate nurture); nor will said party of the second part covet, retain, nor seek to remove any knives, forks, spoons, or other tableware whatsoever; nor is anything said or implied or otherwise intimated in this covenant to be construed as permitting the party of the second part to carry on loud laughter, song, carnival, nor social uproar; nor unnecessarily, further than is tactful for the procurement of expeditious attention, to endear himself to or otherwise cajole, compliment, and ingratiate the waitress.

And Furthermore, that title to said Meal does not pass until the party of the second part has conveyed, of his mansuetude and proper charity, a gratuity, fee, honorarium, lagniappe, pourboire, easement or tip of not less than 15 per cent of the price of said Meal; which easement, while customarily spoken of as a free-will grant or gratuity, is to be constructively regarded as an entail and a necessary encumbrance upon said Meal.

And the said party of the first part covenants with the said party of the second part as follows: That the said C. D. is seized of the said Meal in fee simple, and shall quietly enjoy said Meal subject to the covenants and restrictions and encumbrances hereinbefore set out, subject to the good pleasure of the Head Waiter.

In Witness Whereof these presents are signed,

(LOC. SIG.)

ADVENTURES IN HIGH FINANCE

There is no way in which one can so surely arouse the suspicions of bankers as by trying to put some money in their hands. We went round to a near-by bank hoping to open an account. As we had formerly dealt with an uptown branch of the same institution, and as the cheque we wanted to deposit bore the name of a quite well-known firm, we thought all would be easy. But no; it seemed that there was no convincing way to identify ourself. Hopefully we pulled out a stack of letters, but these were waved aside. We began to feel more and more as though we had come with some sinister intent. We started to light our pipe, and then it occurred to us that perhaps that would be regarded as the gesture of a hardened cracksman, seeking to appear at his ease. We wondered if, in all our motions, we were betraying the suspicious conduct of the professional embezzler. Perhaps the courteous banker was putting us through some Freudian third degree ... in these days when the workings of the unconscious are so shrewdly canvassed, was there anything abominable in the cellar of our soul which we were giving away without realizing ... had we not thought to ourself, as we entered the door, well, this is a fairly decent cheque to start an account with, but we won't keep our balance anywhere near that figure ... perhaps our Freudian banker had spotted that thought and was sending for a psychological patrol wagon ... well, how could we identify ourself? Did we know any one who had an account in that branch? No.

We thought of a friend of ours who banked at another branch of this bank, not far away. The banker called him up and whispered strangely over the phone. We were asked to take off our hat. Apparently our friend was describing us. We hoped that he was saying "stout" rather than "fat." But it seemed that the corroboration of our friend only increased our host's precaution. Perhaps he thought it was a carefully worked-out con game, in which our friend was a confederate. We signed our name several times, on little cards, with a desperate attempt to appear unconcerned. In spite of our best efforts, we could not help thinking that each time we wrote it we must be looking as though we were trying to remember how we had written it the last time. Still the banker hesitated. Then he called up our friend again. He asked him if he would know our voice over the phone. Our friend said he would. We spoke to our friend, with whom we had eaten lunch a few minutes before. He asked, to identify us, what we had had for lunch.

Horrible instant! For a moment we could not remember. The eyes of the banker and his assistant were glittering upon us. Then we spoke glibly enough. "An oyster patty," we said; "two cups of tea, and a rice pudding which we asked for cold, but which was given us hot."

Our friend asserted, to the banker, that we were undeniably us, and indeed the homely particularity of the luncheon items had already made incision in his hardened bosom. He smiled radiantly at us and gave us a cheque book. Then he told us we couldn't draw against our account until the original cheque had passed through the Clearing House, and sent a youth back to the office with us so that we could be unmistakably identified.

As we left the banker's office someone else was ushered in. "Here's another gentleman to open an account," said the assistant. "We hope he knows what he had for lunch," we said to the banker.

ON VISITING BOOKSHOPS

It Is a curious thing that so many people only go into a bookshop when they happen to need some particular book. Do they never drop in for a little innocent carouse and refreshment? There are some knightly souls who even go so far as to make their visits to bookshops a kind of chivalrous errantry at large. They go in not because they need any certain volume, but because they feel that there may be some book that needs them. Some wistful, little forgotten sheaf of loveliness, long pining away on an upper shelf— why not ride up, fling her across your charger (or your charge account), and gallop away. Be a little knightly, you book-lovers!

The lack of intelligence with which people use bookshops is, one supposes, no more flagrant than the lack of intelligence with which we use all the rest of the machinery of civilization. In this age, and particularly in this city, we haven't time to be intelligent.

A queer thing about books, if you open your heart to them, is the instant and irresistible way they follow you with their appeal. You know at once, if you are clairvoyant in these matters (libre-voyant, one might say), when you have met your book. You may dally and evade, you may go on about your affairs, but the paragraph of prose your eye fell upon, or the snatch of verses, or perhaps only the spirit and flavour of the volume, more divined than reasonably noted, will follow you. A few lines glimpsed on a page may alter your whole trend of thought for the day, reverse the currents of the mind, change the profile of the city. The other evening, on a subway car, we were reading Walter de la Mare's interesting little essay about Rupert Brooke. His discussion of children, their dreaming ways, their exalted simplicity and absorption, changed the whole tenor of our voyage by some magical chemistry of thought. It was no longer a wild, barbaric struggle with our fellowmen, but a venture of faith and recompense, taking us home to the bedtime of a child.

The moment when one meets a book and knows, beyond shadow of doubt, that that book must be his—not necessarily now, but some time—is among the happiest excitements of the spirit. An indescribable virtue effuses from some books. One can feel the radiations of an honest book long before one sees it, if one has a sensitive pulse for such affairs. Its honour and truth will speak through the advertising. Its mind and heart will cry out even underneath the extravagance of jacket-blurbings. Some shrewd soul, who understands books, remarked some time ago on the editorial page of the Sun's book review that no superlative on a jacket had ever done the book an atom of good. He was right, as far as the true bookster is concerned. We choose our dinner not by the wrappers, but by the veining and gristle of the meat within. The other day, prowling about a bookshop, we came upon two paper-bound copies of a little book of poems by Alice Meynell. They had been there for at least two years. We had seen them before, a year or more ago, but had not looked into them fearing to be tempted. This time we ventured. We came upon two poems—"To O, Of Her Dark Eyes," and "A Wind of Clear Weather in England." The book was ours—or rather, we were its, though we did not yield at once. We came back the next day and got it. We are still wondering how a book like that could stay in the shop so long. Once we had it, the day was different. The sky was sluiced with a clearer blue, air and sunlight blended for a keener intake of the lungs, faces seen along the street moved us with a livelier shock of interest and surprise. The wind that moved over Sussex and blew Mrs. Meynell's heart into her lines was still flowing across the ribs and ledges of our distant scene.

There is no mistaking a real book when one meets it. It is like falling in love, and like that colossal adventure it is an experience of great social import. Even as the tranced swain, the book-lover yearns to tell others of his bliss. He writes letters about it, adds it to the postscript of all manner of communications, intrudes it into telephone messages, and insists on his friends writing down the title of the find. Like the simple-hearted betrothed, once certain of his conquest, "I want you to love her, too!" It is a jealous passion also. He feels a little indignant if he finds that any one else has discovered the book, too. He sees an enthusiastic review—very likely in The New Republic—and says, with great scorn, "I read the book three months ago." There are even some perversions of passion by which a book-lover loses much of his affection for his pet if he sees it too highly commended by some rival critic.

This sharp ecstasy of discovering books for one's self is not always widespread. There are many who, for one reason or another, prefer to have their books found out for them. But for the complete zealot nothing transcends the zest of pioneering for himself. And therefore working for a publisher is, to a certain type of mind, a never-failing fascination. As H. M. Tomlinson says in "Old Junk," that fascinating collection of sensitive and beautifully poised sketches which came to us recently with a shock of thrilling delight:

> To come upon a craft rigged so, though at her moorings and with sails furled, her slender poles upspringing from the bright plane of a brimming harbour, is to me as rare and sensational a delight as the rediscovery, when idling with a book, of a favourite lyric.

To read just that passage, and the phrase the bright plane of a brimming harbour, is one of those "rare and sensational delights" that set the mind moving on lovely journeys of its own, and mark off visits to a bookshop not as casual errands of reason, but as necessary acts of devotion. We visit bookshops not so often to buy any one special book, but rather to rediscover, in the happier and more expressive words of others, our own encumbered soul.

A DISCOVERY

We are going to tell the truth. It has been on our mind for some time. We are going to tell it exactly, without any balancing or trimming or crimped edges. We are weary of talking about trivialities and are going to come plump and plain to the adventures of our own mind. These are real adventures, just as real as the things we see. The green frog that took refuge on our porch last night was no more real. Perhaps frogs don't care so much for wet as they are supposed to, for when that excellent thunderstorm came along and the ceiling of the night was sheeted with lilac brightness, through which ran quivering threads of naked fire (not just the soft, tame, flabby fire of the domestic hearth, but the real core and marrow of flame, its hungry, terrible, destroying self), our friend the frog came hopping up on the porch where we stood, apparently to take shelter. How brilliant was his black and silver eye when we picked him up! His direct and honourable regard somehow made us feel ashamed, we know not why. And yet we have plenty to be ashamed about—but how did he know? He was still on the porch this morning. Equally real was the catbird on the hedge as we came down toward the station. She—we call her so, for there was unmistakable ladyhood in her delicately tailored trimness—she bickered at us in a cheerful way, on top of those bushes which were so loaded with the night's rainfall that they shone a blurred cobweb gray in the lifting light. Her eye was also dark and polished and lucid, like a bead of ink. It also had the same effect of tribulation on our spirit. Neither the catbird nor the frog, we said to ourself, would have tormented their souls trying to "invent" something to write about. They would have told what happened to them, and let it go at that. So, as we walked along under an arcade of maple trees, admiring the little green seed-biplanes brought down by the thrash of the rain—they look rather as though they would make good coathangers for fairies—we asked ourself why we could not be as straightforward as the bird and the frog, and talk about what was in our mind.

The most exciting thing that happened to us when we got to New York last February was finding a book in a yellow wrapper. Its title was "Old Junk," which appealed to us. The name of the author was H. M. Tomlinson, which immediately became to us a name of honour and great meaning. All day and every day intelligent men find themselves surrounded by oceans of what is quaintly called "reading matter." Most of it is turgid, lumpy, fuzzy in texture, squalid in intellect. The rewards of the literary world—that is, the tangible, potable, spendable rewards—go mostly to the cheapjack and the mountebank. And yet here was a man who in every paragraph spoke to the keenest intellectual sense—who, ten times a page, enchanted the reader with the surprising and delicious pang given by the critically chosen word. We sat up late at night reading that book, marvelling at our good fortune. We wanted to cry aloud (to such as cared to understand), "Rejoice and be exceeding glad, for here is born a man who knows how to write!" In our exuberance we seized a pen and wrote in the stern of our copy: "Here speaks the Lord God of prose; here is the clear eye, the ironic mind, the compassionate heart; the thrilling honesty and (apparent) simplicity of great work." Then we set about making the book known to our friends. We propelled them into bookshops and made them buy it. We took our own copy down to William McFee on S.S. Turrialba and a glad heart was ours when he, too, said it was "the real thing." This is a small matter, you say? When the discovery of an honest pen becomes a small matter life will lose something of its savour. Those who understand will understand; let the others spend their time in the smoker playing pinochle. Those who care about these things can get the book for themselves.

Of Mr. Tomlinson in person: he is a London newspaperman, we understand, and now on the staff of the London Nation. (Trust Mr. Massingham, the editor of that journal, to know an honest writer when he sees him.) Mr. Tomlinson says of himself:

> My life is like my portrait. It won't bear investigation. I am not conscious of having done anything that would interest either a policeman or the young lady of the kind who dotes on Daddy Long Legs; worse luck. It's about time I got down to business and did something interesting either to one or the other. That is why it won't bear investigation, this record of mine. I am about as entertaining as one of the crowd coming out of the factory gates with his full dinner pail. All my adventures have been no more than keeping that pail moderately full. I've been doing that since I was twelve, in all sorts of ways. I was an office boy and a clerk among London's ships, in the last days of the clippers. And I am forced to recall some of the things—such as bookkeeping in a jam factory and stoking on a tramp steamer—I can understand why I and my fellows, without wanting to, drifted about in indecision till we drifted into

45

war and drifted into peace. And of course, I've been a journalist. I am still; and so have seen much of Africa, America, and Europe, without knowing exactly why. I was in France in 1914—the August, too, of that year, and woke up from that nightmare in 1917, after the Vimy Ridge attack, when I returned to England to sit with my wife and children in a cellar whenever it was a fine night and listened to the guns and bombs. God, who knows all, might make something of this sort of inconsequential drift of one day into the next, but I give it up.

But now we pass to the phase of the matter that puzzles us. How is it that there are some books which can never have abiding life until they perish and are born again? We have noticed it so often. There is a book of a certain sort to which this process seems inevitable. One need only mention Leonard Merrick or Samuel Butler as examples. The book, we will suppose, has some peculiar subtlety or flavour of appeal. (We are thinking at the moment of William McFee's "Letters From an Ocean Tramp.") It is published and falls dead. Later on—usually about ten years later—it is taken up with vigour by some other publisher, the stone is rolled away from the sepulchre, and it begins to move among its destined lovers.

This remark is caused by our delighted discovery of a previous book by the author of "Old Junk." "The Sea and the Jungle" is the title of it, the tale of a voyage on the tramp steamer Capella, from Swansea to Para in the Brazils, and thence 2,000 miles along the forests of the Amazon and Madeira rivers. It is the kind of book whose readers will never forget it; the kind of book that happens to some happy writers once in a lifetime (and to many never at all) when the moving hand seems gloriously in gear with the tremulous and busy mind, and all the spinning earth stands hearkeningly still waiting for the perfect expression of the thought. It is the work of a hand trained in laborious task-work and then set magnificently free, for a few blessed months, under no burden save that of putting its captaining spirit truthfully on paper. And this book—in which there is a sea passage that not even Mr. Conrad has ever bettered—this book, which makes the utmost self-satisfied heroics of the Prominent Writers of our market place shrivel uncomfortably in remembrance—this book, we repeat, though published in this country in 1913, has been long out of print; and the copy which we were lucky enough to lay hand on through the courtesy of the State Librarian of Pennsylvania had not previously been borrowed since November 18, 1913. Someone asks us if this man can really write.

Let us choose a paragraph for example. This deals with the first day at sea of the tramp steamer Capella:

> It was December, but by luck we found a halcyon morning which had got lost in the year's procession. It was a Sunday morning, and it had not been ashore. It was still virgin, bearing a vestal light. It had not been soiled yet by any suspicion of this trampled planet, this muddy star, which its innocent and tenuous rays had discovered in the region of night. I thought it still was regarding us as a lucky find there. Its light was tremulous, as if with joy and eagerness. I met this discovering morning as your ambassador while you still slept, and betrayed not, I hope, any grayness and bleared satiety of ours to its pure, frail, and lucid regard. That was the last good service I did before leaving you quite. I was glad to see how well your old earth did meet such a light, as though it had no difficulty in looking day in the face. The world was miraculously renewed. It rose, and received the newborn of Aurora in its arms. There were clouds of pearl above hills of chrysoprase. The sea ran in volatile flames. The shadows on the bright deck shot to and fro as we rolled. The breakfast bell rang not too soon. This was a right beginning.

The above is a paragraph that we have chosen from Mr. Tomlinson's book almost at random. We could spend the whole afternoon (and a happy afternoon it would be for us) copying out for you passages from "The Sea and the Jungle" that would give you the extremity of pleasure, O high-spirited reader! It is an odd thing, it is a quaint thing, it is a thing that would seem inconceivable (were we not tolerably acquainted with the vagaries of the reading public) that a book of this sort should lie perdu on the shelves of a few libraries. Yet one must not leap too heartily to the wrong conclusion. The reading public is avid of good books, but it does not hear about them. Now we would venture to say that we know fifty people—nay, two hundred and fifty—who would never have done thanking us if we could lay a copy of a book of this sort in their hand. They would think it the greatest favour we could do them if we could tell them where they could go and lay down honest money and buy it. And we have to retort that it is out of print, not procurable.[1] Is it the fault of publishers? We do not think so—or not very often. For every

---

[1] Since this was written, a new edition has been published by E. P. Dutton & Co.

47

publisher has experience of this sort of thing—books that he knows to be of extraordinary quality and fascination which simply lie like lead in his stockroom, and people will not listen to what he says about them. Whose fault is it, then? Heaven knows.

SILAS ORRIN HOWES

There died in New York, on February 11, 1918, one who perhaps as worthily as any man in any age represented the peculiar traits and charms of the book-lover, a man whose personal loveliness was only equalled by his unassuming modesty, a man who was an honour to the fine old profession of bookselling.

There will be some who frequent Brentano's bookstore in New York who will long remember the quiet little gentleman who held the post nearest the front door, whose face lit with such a gentle and gracious smile when he saw a friend approach, who endured with patience and courtesy the thousand small annoyances that every salesman knows. There were encounters with the bourgeois customer, there were the exhausting fatigues of the rush season, there were the day-long calls on the slender and none too robust frame. But through it all he kept the perfect and unassuming grace of the high-born gentleman he was. An old-fashioned courtesy and gallantry moved in his blood.

It was an honour to know Silas Orrin Howes, and some have been fortunate to have disclosed to them the richness and simple bravery of that lover of truth and beauty. The present writer was one of the least and latest of these. Twice, during the last months of his life, it was my very good fortune to spend an evening with him at his room on Lexington Avenue, to drink the delicious coffee he brewed in his percolator given him by William Marion Reedy, to mull with him over the remarkable scrap-books he had compiled out of the richness of his varied reading, and to hear him talk about books and life.

Silas Orrin Howes was born in Macon, Georgia, October 15, 1867. He attended school in Macon and Atlanta, and then in Franklin, Indiana. He never went to college.

When he was born, a passion for books was born with him. His niece tells me that by the time he was twenty-one he had collected a considerable library. He began life as a newspaper man, on the Macon Telegraph. About the age of twenty-four he went to Galveston where he was first a copy-reader, and then for seven years telegraph editor of the Galveston News.

I do not know all the details of his life in Galveston, where he lived for about twenty years. He told me that at the time of the disastrous storm and flood he was working in a drug store near the Gulf front. He gave me a thrilling description of the night he spent standing on the prescription counter with the water swirling about his waist. He slept in a little room at the back of the store, where he had a shelf of books which were particularly dear to him. Among them was a volume of Henley's poems. When the flood subsided all the books were gone, but the next day as he was looking over the wreckage of neighbouring houses he found his Henley washed up on a doorstep—covered with slime and filth but still intact. He sent it to Brentano's in New York to be rebound in vellum, instructing them not to clean it in any way. He wrote to Henley about the incident, who sent him a very friendly autographed card which he pasted in the volume. That was one of the books which he held most dear, and rightly.

I do not know just when he came to New York; about 1910, I believe. He took a position as salesman at Brentano's. After a couple of years there he became anxious to try the book business on his own account. He and his nephew opened a shop in San Antonio. Neither of them had much real business experience. Certainly Howes himself was far too devoted a book-lover to be a good business man! After a few months the venture ended in failure, and all the personal library which he had collected through patient years was swallowed up in the disaster. After this he returned to Brentano's, where he remained until his death. About a year before his death he was run over by a taxicab, which shook his nerves a great deal.

At some time during his career he came into intimate friendly contact with Ambrose Bierce, and used to tell many entertaining anecdotes about that erratic venturer in letters. He edited one of Bierce's volumes, adding a pleasant and scholarly little introduction. He was an occasional contributor to Reedy's Mirror, where he enjoyed indulging in his original vein of satire and shrewd comment. He was a great lover of quaint and exotic restaurants, and was particularly fond of the Turkish café, the Constantinople, just off Madison Square. It was a treat to go there with him, see him summon the waiter by clapping his hands (in the eastern fashion), and enjoy the strangely compounded dishes of that queer menu. He had sampled every Bulgar, Turkish, Balkan, French, and Scandinavian restaurant on Lexington Avenue. His taste in unusual and savoury dishes was as characteristic as his love for the finer flavours of literature. I remember last November I elicited from him that he had never tasted gooseberry jam, and had a jolly time

50

hunting for a jar, which I found at last at Park and Tilford's, although the sales-girl protested there was no such thing. I took it to him and made him promise to eat it at his breakfasts.

He had the true passions of the book-lover, which are not allotted to many. He had read hungrily, enjoying chiefly those magical draughts of prose which linger in the mind: Bacon, Sir Thomas Browne, Pater, Thoreau, Conrad. He was much of a recluse, a little saddened and sharpened perhaps by some of his experiences; and he loved, above all, those writers who can present truth with a faint tang of acid flavour, the gooseberry jam of literature as it were. One of my last satisfactions was to convert him (in some measure) to an enthusiasm for Pearsall Smith's "Trivia."

As one looks back at that quiet, honourable life, one is aware of a high, noble spirit shining through it: a spirit that sought but little for itself, welcomed love and comradeship that came its way, and was content with a modest round of routine duty because it afforded inner contact with what was beautiful and true. One remembers an innate gentleness, and a loyalty to a high and chivalrous ideal.

Such a life might be a lesson, if anything could, to the bumptious and "efficient" and smug. Time after time I have watched him serving some furred and jewelled customer who was not fit to exchange words with him; I have seen him jostled in a crowded aisle by some parvenu ignoramus who knew not that this quiet little man was one of the immortal spirits of gentleness and breeding who associate in quiet hours with the unburied dead of English letters. That corner of the store, near the front door, can never be the same.

Such a life could only fittingly be described by the gentle, inseeing pen of an E. V. Lucas.

My greatest regret and disappointment, when I heard of his sudden death, was that he would never know of a little tribute I had paid him in a forthcoming book. I had been saving it as a surprise for him, for I knew it would please him. And now he will never know.

February, 1918.

JOYCE KILMER

I

I wonder if there is any other country where the death of a young poet is double-column front-page news?

And if poets were able to proofread their own obits, I wonder if any two lines would have given Joyce Kilmer more honest pride than these:

> JOYCE KILMER, POET,
> IS KILLED IN ACTION

which gave many hearts a pang when they picked up the newspaper last Sunday morning.

Joyce Kilmer died as he lived—"in action." He found life intensely amusing, unspeakably interesting; his energy was unlimited, his courage stout. He attacked life at all points, rapidly gathered its complexities about him, and the more intricate it became the more zestful he found it. Nothing bewildered him, nothing terrified. By the time he was thirty he had attained an almost unique position in literary circles. He lectured on poetry, he interviewed famous men of letters, he was poet, editor, essayist, critic, anthologist. He was endlessly active, full of delightful mirth and a thousand schemes for outwitting the devil of necessity that hunts all brainworkers. Nothing could quench him. He was ready to turn out a poem, an essay, a critical article, a lecture, at a few minutes' notice. He had been along all the pavements of Grub Street, perhaps the most exciting place of breadwinning known to the civilized man. From his beginning as a sales clerk in a New York bookstore (where, so the tale goes, by misreading the price cipher he sold a $150 volume for $1.50) down to the time when he was run over by an Erie train and dictated his weekly article for the New York Times in hospital with three broken ribs, no difficulties or perplexities daunted him.

But beneath this whirling activity which amused and amazed his friends there lay a deeper and quieter vein which was rich in its own passion. It is not becoming to prate of what lies in other men's souls; we all have our secrecies and sanctuaries, rarely acknowledged even to ourselves. But no one can read Joyce Kilmer's poems without grasping his vigorous idealism, his keen sense of beauty, his devout and simple religion, his clutch on the preciousness of common things. He loved the precarious bustle on Grub Street; he was of that adventurous, buoyant stuff that rejects hum-drum security and a pelfed and padded life. He always insisted that America is the very shrine and fountain of poetry, and this country (which is indeed pathetically eager to take poets to its bosom) stirred his vivid imagination. The romance of the commuter's train and the suburban street, of the delicatessen shop and the circus and the snowman in the yard—these were the familiar themes where he was rich and felicitous. Many a commuter will remember his beautiful poem "The 12:45," bespeaking the thrill we have all felt in the shabby midnight train that takes us home, yearning and weary, to the well-beloved hearth:

> What love commands, the train fulfills
> And beautiful upon the hills
> Are these our feet of burnished steel.
> Subtly and certainly, I feel
> That Glen Rock welcomes us to her.
> And silent Ridgewood seems to stir
> And smile, because she knows the train
> Has brought her children back again.
> We carry people home—and so
> God speeds us, wheresoe'er we go.
> The midnight train is slow and old,
> But of it let this thing be told,
> To its high honour be it said,
> It carries weary folk to bed.

To a man such as this, whose whole fervent and busy adventure was lit within by the lamplight and firelight of domestic passion, the war, with its broken homes and defiled sanctities, came as a personal affront. Both to his craving for the glamour of such a colossal drama, and to his sense of what was most worshipful in human life, the call was irresistible. Counsels of prudence and comfort were as nothing; the heart-shaking poetry of this nation's entry into an utterly unselfish war burned away all barriers. His life had been a fury of writing, but those who thought he had entered the war merely to make journalism about it were mistaken. Only a few weeks before his death he wrote:

> To tell the truth, I am not interested in writing nowadays, except in so far as writing is the expression of something

53

beautiful. And I see daily and nightly the expression of beauty in action instead of words, and I find it more satisfactory. I am a sergeant in the regimental intelligence section—the most fascinating work possible—more thrills in it than in any other branch, except, possibly, aviation. Wonderful life! But I don't know what I'll be able to do in civilian life—unless I become a fireman!

As journalist and lecturer Kilmer was copious and enthusiastic rather than deep. He found—a good deal to his own secret mirth—women's clubs and poetry societies sitting earnestly at his feet, expectant to hear ultimate truth on deep matters. His humour prompted him to give them the ultimate truth they craved. If his critical judgments were not always heavily documented or long pondered, they were entertaining and pleasantly put. The earnest world of literary societies and blue-hosed salons lay about his feet; he flashed in it merrily, chuckling inwardly as he found hundreds of worthy people hanging breathless on his words. A kind of Kilmer cult grew apace; he had his followers and his devotees. I mention these things because he would have been the first to chuckle over them. I do not think he would want to be remembered as having taken all that sort of thing too seriously. It was all a delicious game—part of the grand joke of living. Sometimes, among his friends, he would begin to pontificate in his platform manner. Then he would recall himself, and his characteristic grin would flood his face.

As a journalist, I say, he was copious; but as a poet his song was always prompted by a genuine gush of emotion. "A poet is only a glorified reporter," he used to say; he took as his favourite assignment the happier precincts of the human heart. As he said of Belloc, a true poet will never write to order—not even to his own order. He sang because he heard life singing all about him. His three little books of poems have always been dear to lovers of honest simplicity. And now their words will be lit henceforward by an inner and tender brightness—the memory of a gallant boy who flung himself finely against the walls of life. Where they breached he broke through and waved his sword laughing. Where they hurled him back he turned away, laughing still.

II

Kilmer wrote from France, in answer to an inquiry as to his ideas about poetry, "All that poetry can be expected to do is to give pleasure of a noble sort to its readers." He might have said "pleasure or pain of a noble sort."

It is both pleasure and pain, of a very noble sort, that the reader will find in Robert Cortes Holliday's memoir, which introduces the two volumes of Kilmer's poems, essays, and letters. The ultimate and eloquent tribute to Kilmer's rich, brave, and jocund personality is that it has raised up so moving a testament of friendship. Mr. Holliday's lively and tender essay is worthy to stand among the great memorials of brotherly affection that have enriched our speech. To say that Kilmer was not a Keats is not to say that the friendship that irradiates Mr. Holliday's memoir was less lovely than that of Keats and Severn, for instance. The beauty of any human intercourse is not measured by the plane on which it moves.

Pleasure and pain of a noble sort are woven in every fibre of this sparkling casting-up of the blithe years. Pleasure indeed of the fullest, for the chronicle abounds in the surcharged hilarity and affectionate humour that we have grown to expect in any matters connected with Joyce Kilmer. The biographer dwells with loving and smiling particularity on the elvish phases of the young knight-errant. It is by the very likeness of his tender and glowing portrait that we find pleasure overflowing into pain—into a wincing recognition of destiny's unriddled ways with men. This memory was written out of a full heart, with the poignance that lies in every backward human gaze. It is only in the backward look that the landscape's contours lie revealed in their true form and perspective. It is only when we have lost what was most dear that we know fully what it meant. That is Fate's way with us: it cannot be amended.

There will be no need for the most querulous appraiser to find fault with Mr. Holliday on the score of over-eulogy. He does not try to push sound carpentry or ready wit into genius. Fortune and his own impetuous onslaught upon life cast Kilmer into the rôle of hack journalist: he would have claimed no other title. Yet he adorned Grub Street (that most fascinating of all thorny ways) with gestures and music of his own. Out of his glowing and busy brain he drew matter that was never dull, never bitter or petty or slovenly. In the fervent attack and counter-attack, shock and counter-shock of his strenuous days he never forgot his secret loyalty to fine craftsmanship. He kept half a dozen brightly coloured balls spinning in air at all times—verses, essays, reviews, lectures, introductions, interviews, anthologies, and what-not; yet each of these was deftly done. When he went to France and his days of hack work were over, when the necessities of life no longer threatened him, the journalistic habit fell away. It was never more than a garment, worn gracefully, but still only what the tailors call a business suit.

In France, Kilmer wrote but a handful of pieces intended for publication, but at least one of them—the prose sketch "Holy Ireland"—showed his essential fibre. The comparative silence of his pen when he found himself face to face with war was a true expression. It bespoke the decent idealism that underlay the combats of a journalist wringing a living out of the tissues of a busy brain. The tender humour and quaint austerity of his homeward letters exhibit the man at his inmost. What could better the imaginative genius of the phrase in which he speaks of friendship developed by common dangers and hardships as "a fine, hearty, roaring, mirthful sort of thing, like an open fire of whole pine trees in a giant's castle?"

The memoir and Kilmer's own letters admit us to see something of the spiritual phases of this man's life, whose soul found "happiness and quiet kind" in the Roman Catholic faith. The most secret strengths and weaknesses that govern men's lives are strangely unknown to many of their intimates: one wonders how many of Kilmer's associates on the Times staff knew of his habit of stopping daily at the Church of the Holy Innocents, near the newspaper office, to pray. It was the sorrow of personal affliction that brought Kilmer to the Catholic Church. Shortly after being received into that communion he wrote:

> Just off Broadway on the way from the Hudson Tube Station to the Times Building, there is a church called the Church of the Holy Innocents. Since it is in the heart of the Tenderloin, this name is strangely appropriate—for there surely is need of youth and innocence. Well, every morning for months I stopped on my way to the office and prayed in this church for faith. When faith did come, it came, I think, by way of my little paralyzed daughter. Her lifeless hands led me; I think her tiny feet still know beautiful paths.

Mr. Holliday does well to point out that Kilmer was almost unique in this country as a representative of the Bellocian School of Catholic journalism, in which piety and mirth dwell so comfortably together; though he might have mentioned T. A. Daly as an older and subtler master of devout merriment, dipping in his own inkwell rather than in any imported bottles. It is to Belloc, of course, and to Gilbert Chesterton, that one must go to learn the secret of Kilmer's literary manner. Yet, as Holliday affirms, the similarity is due as much to an affinity of mind with these Englishmen as to any eagerness to imitate. Kilmer was like them in being essentially a humorist. One glance at his face, with its glowing red-brown eyes (the colour of port wine), and the twitching in-drawn corners of the mouth, gave the observer an impression of benignant drollery. Mr. Holliday well says: "People have made very creditable reputations as humorists who never wrote anything like as humorous essays as those of Joyce Kilmer. They fairly reek with the joy of life."

"He that lives by the pen shall perish by the pen," the biographer tells us, quoting James Huneker. "For a sapling poet, within a few short years and by the hard business of words, to attain to a secretary and a butler and a family of, at length, four children, is a modern Arabian Nights Tale." Aye, indeed! But Joyce Kilmer will have as genuine a claim on remembrance by reason of his friends' love as in anything his own hand penned. And what an encircling, almost paternal, gentleness there is in the picture of the young poet as a salesman at Scribner's bookstore:

> His smile, never far away, when it came was winning, charming. It broke like spring sunshine, it was so fresh and warm and clear. And there was noticeable then in his eyes a light, a quiet glow, which marked him as a spirit not to be forgotten. So tenderly boyish was he in effect that his confrères among the book clerks accepted with difficulty the story that he was married. When it was told that he had a son they gasped their incredulity. And when one day this extraordinary elfin sprite remarked that at the time of his honeymoon he had had a beard they felt (I remember) that the world was without power to astonish them further.

And even more striking is what is implied in the narrative: that when this "elfin sprite," this gently nurtured young man of bookish pursuits, took up the art of war, he gloried in his association with a rip-roaring regiment recruited mainly from hard-handed fellows of the type we may call (with no atom of disrespect) roughnecks.

Hardships and exertions familiar to them were new to him, but he set himself to win their love and respect, and did so. He was not content until he had found his way into the most exhausting and hazardous branch of the whole job. He said, again and again, that he would rather be a sergeant with the 69th than a lieutenant with any other outfit. There was a heart of heroism in the "elfin sprite." The same dashing insouciance that dictated the weekly article for his paper when in hospital with three broken ribs after being run down by a train was hardened and steeled in the sergeant who nightly tore his uniform into ribbons by crawling out through the barbed wire.

Laughter and comradeship and hearty meals clustered about Kilmer: wherever he touched the grindstone of life there flew up a merry shower of sparks. There is convincing testimony to the courage and beauty that lay quiet at the heart of this singer who said that the poet is only a glorified reporter, and wished he had written "Casey at the Bat."

Let us spare his memory the glib and customary dishonesty that says "He died as he would have wished to." No man wishes to die— at least, no poet does. To part with the exhilarating bustle and tumult, the blueness of the sky, the sunlight that tingles on well-known street corners, the plumber's bills and the editor's checks, the mirths of fellowship and the joys of homecoming when lamps are lit—all this is too close a fibre to be stripped easily from the naked heart. But the poet must go where the greatest songs are singing. Perhaps he finds, after all, that life and death are part of the same rhyme.

TALES OF TWO CITIES

I

PHILADELPHIA

AN EARLY TRAIN

The course of events has compelled me for several months to catch an early train at Broad Street three times a week. I call it an "early" train, but, of course, these matters are merely relative; 7:45 are the figures illuminated over the gateway—not so very precocious, perhaps; but quite rathe enough for one of Haroun-al-Raschid temper, who seldom seeks the "oblivion of repose" (Boswell's phrase) before 1 a. m.

Nothing is more pathetic in human nature than its faculty of self-deception. Winding up the alarm clock (the night before) I meditate as to the exact time to elect for its disturbing buzz. If I set it at 6:30 that will give me plenty of time to shave and reach the station with leisure for a pleasurable cup of coffee. But (so frail is the human will) when I wake at 6:30 I will think to myself, "There is plenty of time," and probably turn over for "another five minutes." This will mean a hideous spasm of awakening conscience about 7:10—an unbathed and unshaven tumult of preparation, malisons on the shoe manufacturers who invented boots with eyelets all the way up, a frantic sprint to Sixteenth Street and one of those horrid intervals that shake the very citadel of human reason when I ponder whether it is safer to wait for a possible car or must start hotfoot for the station at once. All this is generally decided by setting the clock for 6:50. Then, if I am spry, I can be under way by 7:20 and have a little time to be philosophical at the corner of Sixteenth and Pine. Of the vile seizures of passion that shake the bosom when a car comes along, seems about to halt, and then passes without stopping—of the spiritual scars these crises leave on the soul of the victim, I cannot trust myself to speak. It does not always happen, thank

59

goodness. One does not always have to throb madly up Sixteenth, with head retorted over one's shoulder to see if a car may still be coming, while the legs make what speed they may on sliddery paving. Sometimes the car does actually appear and one buffets aboard and is buried in a brawny human mass. There is a stop, and one wonders fiercely whether a horse is down ahead, and one had better get out at once and run for it. Tightly wedged in the heart of the car, nothing can be seen. It is all very nerve-racking, and I study, for quietness of mind, the familiar advertising card of the white-bearded old man announcing "It is really very remarkable that a cigar of this quality can be had for seven cents."

Suppose, however, that fortune is with me. I descend at Market Street, and the City Hall dial, shining softly in the fast paling blue of morning, marks 7:30. Now I begin to enjoy myself. I reflect on the curious way in which time seems to stand still during the last minutes before the departure of a train. The half-hour between 7 and 7:30 has vanished in a gruesome flash. Now follow fifteen minutes of exquisite dalliance. Every few moments I look suddenly and savagely at the clock to see if it can be playing some saturnine trick. No, even now it is only 7:32. In the lively alertness of the morning mind a whole wealth of thought and accurate observation can be crammed into a few seconds. I halt for a moment at the window of that little lunchroom on Market Street (between Sixteenth and Fifteenth) where the food comes swiftly speeding from the kitchen on a moving belt. I wonder whether to have breakfast there. It is such fun to see a platter of pale yellow scrambled eggs sliding demurely beside the porcelain counter and whipped dextrously off in front of you by the presiding waiter. But the superlative coffee of the Broad Street Station lunch counter generally lures me on.

What mundane joy can surpass the pleasure of approaching the station lunch counter, with full ten minutes to satisfy a morning appetite! "Morning, colonel," says the waiter, recognizing a steady customer. "Wheatcakes and coffee," you cry. With one deft gesture, it seems, he has handed you a glass brimming with ice water and spread out a snowy napkin. In another moment here is the coffee, with the generous jug of cream. You splash in a large lump of ice to make it cool enough to drink. Perhaps the seat next you is empty, and you put your books and papers on it, thus not having to balance them gingerly on your knees. All round you is a lusty savour of satisfaction, the tinkle of cash registers, napkins fluttering and flashing across the counters, coloured waiters darting to and fro, great clouds of steam rising where the big dish covers are raised on the cooking tables. You see the dark-brown coffee gently quivering in the glass gauge of the nickel boiler. Then here come the wheatcakes. Nowhere else on earth, I firmly believe, are they cooked to just that correct delicacy of golden brown colour; nowhere else are they so soft and light of texture, so hot, so beautifully overlaid with a smooth, almost intangible suggestion of crispness. Two golden butter pats salute the eye, and a jug of syrup. It is now 7:38.

As everyone knows, the correct thing is to start immediately on the first cake, using only syrup. The method of dealing with the other two is classic. One lifts the upper one and places a whole pat of butter on the lower cake. Then one replaces the upper cake upon the lower, leaving the butter to its fate. In that hot and enviable embrace the butter liquefies and spreads itself, gently anointing the field of coming action. Upon the upper shield one smilingly distributes the second butter pat, knifed off into small slices for greater speed of melting. By the time the first cake has been eaten, with the syrup, the other two will be ready for manifest destiny. The butter will be docile and submissive. Now, after again making sure of the time (7:40) the syrup is brought into play and the palate has the congenial task of determining whether the added delight of melting butter outweighs the greater hotness and primal thrill of the first cake which was glossed with the syrup only. You drain your coffee to the dregs; gaze pityingly on those rushing in to snap up a breakfast before the 8 o'clock leaves for New York, pay your check, and saunter out to the train. It is 7:43.

This, to be sure, is only the curtain-raiser to the pleasures to follow. This has been a physical and carnal pleasure. Now follow delights of the mind. In the great gloomy shed wafts and twists of thick steam are jetting upward, heavily coiled in the cold air. In the train you smoke two pipes and read the morning paper. Then you are set down at Haverford. It is like a fairyland of unbelief. Trees and shrubbery are crusted and sheathed in crystal, lucid like chandeliers in the flat, thin light. Along the fence, as you go up the hill, you marvel at the scarlet berries in the hedge, gleaming through the glassy ribs of the bushes. The old willow tree by the Conklin gate is etched against the sky like a Japanese drawing—it has a curious greenish colour beneath that gray sky. There is some mystery in all this. It seems more beautiful than a merely mortal earth vexed by sinful men has any right to be. There is some ice palace in Hans Andersen which is something like it. In a little grove, the boughs, bent down with their shining glaziery, creak softly as they sway in

61

the moving air. The evergreens are clotted with lumps and bags of transparent icing, their fronds sag to the ground. A pale twinkling blueness sifts over distant vistas. The sky whitens in the south and points of light leap up to the eye as the wind turns a loaded branch.

A certain seriousness of demeanour is noticeable on the generally unfurrowed brows of student friends. Midyears are on and one sees them walking, freighted with precious and perishable erudition, toward the halls of trial. They seem a little oppressed with care, too preoccupied to relish the entrancing pallor of this crystallized Eden. One carries, gravely, a cushion and an alarm clock. Not such a bad theory of life, perhaps—to carry in the crises of existence a cushion of philosophy and an alarum of resolution.

RIDGE AVENUE

One of the odd things about human beings is, that wherever they happen to live they accept it as a matter of course. In various foreign cities I have often been amused (as every traveller has) to see people going about their affairs just as though it were natural and unquestionable for them to be there. It is just the same at home. Everyone I see on the streets seems to be not at all amazed at living here instead of (let us say) Indianapolis or Nashville. I envy my small Urchin his sense of the extreme improbability of everything. When he gets on a trolley car he draws a long breath and looks around in ecstasy at the human scenery. I am teaching him to say in a loud, clear tone, as he gets on the car, "Look at all the human beings!" in the same accent of amazement that he uses when he goes to the Zoo. Perhaps in this way he will preserve the happy faculty of being surprised.

It is an agreeable thing to keep the same sense of surprise in one's home town that one would have in a strange city. You will find much to startle you if you keep your eyes open. Yesterday, for instance, I was lucky enough to meet a gentleman who had stood only a few feet away from Lincoln when he made the Gettysburg Speech. Then I found that in a certain cafeteria which I frequent the price you pay for your lunch is always just one cent less than that punched on the check. The cashier explained that this always gives a pleasant surprise to the customers, and has proved such a good advertising dodge that the proprietor made it a habit. And I saw, in a clothing dealer's window on Ninth Street, some fuzzy caps for men, mottled purple and ochre, that proved that the adventurous spirit has not died in the breast of the male sex.

There is much to exercise the eye in a voyage along Ridge Avenue. Approaching by way of Ninth Street, one sees in the window of a barber shop the new contract that the employing barbers have drawn up with their journeymen. This agreement shows a sound sense of human equities, proclaiming as it does that "the owner must not do no act to injure the barber personal earnings." It suddenly occurred to me, what I had not thought of before, how the barbers of Great Britain must have grieved when a London newspaper got up (some years ago) an agitation in favour of every man in England raising a beard in memory of King Edward. The plan was that the money thus saved was to be devoted to building—I had almost said "growing"—a battleship, to be named after the Merry Monarch. Of course, one should not speak of raising a beard, but of lowering it. However——

Ridge Avenue begins at Ninth and Vine, in a mood of depression. Perhaps the fact that it runs out toward the city's greatest collection of cemeteries has made it morbidly conscious of human perishability. At any rate, it starts among pawnshops, old clothing and furniture, and bottles of Old Virginia Bitters, the Great Man Restorer. The famous National Theatre at Callowhill Street has become a garage; it is queer to see the old proscenium arch and gilded ceiling dustily vaulted over a fleet of motortrucks. After a wilderness of railway yards one comes to a curious bit in the 1100 block; a little brick tunnel that bends around into a huddle of backyards and small houses, where a large green parrot was stooping and nodding on a pile of old boxes. This little scene is overlooked by the tall brown spires of the Church of the Assumption on Spring Garden Street.

There is matter for tarrying at the Spring Garden Street crossing. Here is an ambitious fountain built by the bequest of Mary Rebecca Darby Smith, with the carving by J. J. Boyle picturing another Rebecca (she of Genesis xxiv, 14) giving a drink to Abraham's servant and his camels. It is carved in the bronze that the donor gave the fountain "To refresh the weary and thirsty, both man and beast," so it is disconcerting to find it dry, as dry as the inns along the way. The horse trough is boarded over and thirsting equines go up to Broad Street for a draught. The seat by the fountain was occupied by a man reading the New York Journal, always a depressing sight.

Across from the fountain is one of the best magazine and stationery shops in the city. Here I overheard a conversation which I reproduce textually. "What you doing, reading?" said one to another. "Yes, reading about the biggest four-flusher in the Yew-nited States," said he, looking over an afternoon paper which had just come in. "Who do you mean?" "Penrose. Say if it was a Republican in the White House, theyda passed the treaty long ago." The proprietor of this shop is a humorist. Someone came in asking for a certain brand of cigarettes. He does not sell tobacco. "Next door," he said, and added: "And you'll find some over on the fountain."

Ridge Avenue specializes in tobacco shops, where you will find many brands that require a strong head. Red Snapper, Panhandle

64

Scrap, Pinch Hit, Red Horse, Brown's Mule, Jolly Tar, Penn Statue Cuttings, Nickel Cross Cut, Cotton Ball Twist. In the shop windows you will see those photographs illustrating current events, the two favourites just now being a picture of Mike Gilhooley, the famous stowaway, gazing plaintively at the profile of New York, and "Jack Dempsey Goes the Limit," where Jack signs up for a $1,000 war-savings certificate. One wonders if Jack's kind of warfare is really so profitable after all.

There are a number of little side excursions from the avenue that repay scrutiny. Lemon Street, for instance, where in a lane of old brown wooden houses some children were playing in an empty wagon, with the rounded tower of the Rodef Shalom synagogue looming in the background. Best of all is Melon Street and its modest tributary, Park Avenue—stretches of quiet little brick homes with green and yellow shutters and mottled gray marble steps. These little houses have the serene and sunny air so typical of Philadelphia byways. Through their narrow side entrances one sees glimpses of green in backyards. In the front windows move the gently swaying faces of grandmothers, lulled in the to and fro of a rocking chair. There are shining brass knobs and bell-pulls; rubber plants on the sills, or perhaps a small bowl of goldfish with a white china swan floating. In one window was a sign "Vacancies." Over it hung a faded service flag with a golden star. Who could phrase the pathos of these two things, side by side?

At Broad Street, Ridge Avenue leaps up with a spurt of high life. In the window of a hotel dining room a gentleman sat eating his lunch, stevedoring a buttered roll with such gusto that one felt tempted to applaud. There are the white pillars of a bank and the battleship gray of the Salvation Army headquarters. Beyond Broad, the avenue spruces up a bit and enters upon a vivacious phase. Dogs are frequent: white bull terriers lie sunning in the shop windows. Offers to lend money are enticing. There is a fascinating slate yard at 1525, where great gray slabs lie in the sun, a temptation to urchins with a bit of chalk. In the warm bask of the afternoon there rises a pleasing aroma of fruits and vegetables piled up in baskets and crates on the pavement. Grapes give off a delectable savour in the golden air. Elderly ladies are out in force to do the marketing, and their eyes are bright with the bargaining passion. Round the windows of a ten-cent store, most fascinating of all human spectacles, they congregate and compare notes. A fruit dealer has an ingenious stunt to attract attention. On his cash register lies a weird-looking rotund little fish—a butter fish, he calls it—which has a face not unlike that of

Fatty Arbuckle. Either this fish inflates itself or he has blown it full of air in some ingenious manner, for it presents a grotesque appearance, and many ladies stop to inquire. Then he spoofs them gently. "Sure," he says, "it's a jitney fish. It lives on the cash register. It can fly, it can bite, it can talk, and it likes money."

At the corner of Wylie Street stands an old gray house with a mansard roof and gable windows. Against it is a vivid store of fruit glowing in the sun, red and purple and yellow. Here, or on Vineyard Street, one turns off to enter the quaint triangular settlement of Francisville.

THE UNIVERSITY AND THE URCHIN

Sunday afternoon is by old tradition dedicated to the taking of Urchins out to taste the air, and indeed there is no more agreeable pastime. And so, as the Urchin sat in his high chair and thoughtfully shovelled his spoon through meat chopped remarkably small and potatoes mashed in that curious fashion that produces a mass of soft, curly tendrils, his curators discussed the question of where he should be taken.

It was the first Sunday in March—mild and soft and tinctured with spring. "There's the botanic garden at the University," I suggested. The Urchin settled it by rattling his spoon on the plate and sliding several inches of potato into his lap. "Go see garden!" he cried. With the generous tastes of twenty-seven months he cares very little where he is taken; he can find fascination in anything; but something about the word "garden" seemed to allure him. So a little later when he had been duly habited in brown leggings, his minute brown overcoat, and white hat with ribbons behind it, he and his curators set out. The Urchin was in excellent spirits, for he had been promised a ride on a trolley car—a glorious adventure. In one pocket he carried his private collection of talismans, including a horse-chestnut and a picture of a mouse. Also, against emergencies, a miniature handkerchief with a teddy bear embroidered in one corner and a safety pin. The expedition may be deemed to have been a success, as none of these properties were called upon or even remembered.

The car we boarded did not take us just where we expected to go, but that made little difference to the Urchin, who gazed steadfastly out of the window at a panorama of shabby streets, and offered no comment except one of extreme exultation when we passed a large poster of a cow. Admirably docile, he felt confident that the unusual conjunction of both arbiters of destiny and an impressive trolley car would in the end produce something extremely worth while. We sped across Gray's Ferry bridge—it seems strange to think that region was once so quiet, green, and rustic—transferred to another car on Woodland Avenue, past the white medley of tombstones in Woodland Cemetery, and got off at the entrance to the dormitory quadrangles at Thirty-seventh Street. We entered through the archway—the Urchin's first introduction to an academic atmosphere. "This is the University," I said to him severely, and he was much impressed. As is his way, he conducted himself with extreme sobriety until he should get the hang of this new experience and see what it was all about. I knew from the serene gold sparkle of his brown eyes that there was plenty of larking spirit in him, waiting until he knew whether it was safe to give it play. He held my hand punctiliously while waiting to see what manner of place this University was.

A college quadrangle on a Sunday afternoon has a feeling all its own. Thin tinklings of mandolins eddy from open windows, in which young men may be seen propped up against bright-coloured cushions, always smoking, and sometimes reading with an apparent zeal which might deceive a few onlookers. But the slightest sound of footfalls on the pavement outside their rooms causes these heads to turn and scan the passers. There is always a vague hope in these youthful breasts that some damsel of notable fairness may have strayed within the bastions. Groups of ladies of youth and beauty do often walk demurely through the courts, and may be sure of hearing admiring whistles shrilled through the sunny air. When a lady walks through a college quadrangle and hears no sibilation, let her know sadly that first youth is past. Even the sedate guardianship of Scribe and Urchin did not forfeit one Lady of Destiny her proper homage of tuneful testimonial. So be it ever!

One who inhabited college quadrangles not so immeasurably long ago, and remembers with secret pain how massively old, experienced, and worldly wise he then thought himself, can never resist a throb of amazement at the entertaining youthfulness of these young monks. How quaintly juvenile they are, and how oddly that assumption of grave superiority sits upon their golden brows! With what an inimitable air of wisdom, cynicism, anciently, learned aloofness and desire to be observed do they stroll to and fro across the quads, so keenly aware in their inmost bosoms of the presence of visitors and determined to grant an appearance of mingled wisdom, great age, and sad doggishness! What a devil-may-care swing to the stride, what a nonchalance in the perpetual wreath of cigarette smoke, what a carefully assumed bearing of one carrying great wisdom lightly and easily casting it aside for the moment in the pursuit of some waggish trifle. "Here," those very self-conscious young visages seem to betray, "is one who might tell you all about the Holy Roman Empire, and yet is, for the moment, diverting himself with a mere mandolin." And yet, as the Lady of Destiny shrewdly observed, it is a pity they should mar their beautiful quadrangles with orange peel and scraps of paper.

68

We walked for some time through those stately courts of Tudor brick and then passed down the little inclined path to the botanic garden, where irises and fresh green spikes are already pushing up through the damp earth. A pale mellow sunlight lay upon the gravel walks and the Urchin resumed his customary zeal. He ran here and there along the byways, examined the rock borders with an air of scientific questioning, and watched the other children playing by the muddy pond. We found shrubbery swelling with buds, also flappers walking hatless and blanched with talcum, accompanied by Urchins of a larger growth. Both these phenomena we took to be a sign of the coming equinox.

Returning to the dormitory quadrangles, we sat down on a wooden bench to rest, while the Urchin, now convinced that a university is nothing to be awed by, scampered about on the turf. His eye was a bright jewel of roguishness, for he thought that in trotting about the grass he was doing something supremely wicked. He has been carefully trained not to err on the grass of the city square to which he is best accustomed, so this surprising and unchecked revelry quite went to his head. Across and about those wide plots of sodden turf he trotted and chuckled, a small, quaint mortal with his hat ribbons fluttering. Cheering whistles hailed him from open windows above, and he smiled to himself with grave dignity. Apparently, like a distinguished statesman, he regarded these tributes not as meant for himself, but for the great body of childhood he innocently represents, and indeed from which his applauders are not so inextricably severed. With the placid and unconscious happiness of a puppy he careered and meandered, without motive or method. Perhaps his underlying thought of a university, if he has any, is that it is a place where no one says "Keep Off the Grass," and, intellectually speaking, that would not be such a bad motto for an institution of learning.

I don't know whether Doctor Tait McKenzie so intended it, but his appealing and beautiful statue of Young Franklin in front of the University gymnasium is admirably devised for the delight of small Urchins. While their curators take pleasure in the bronze itself, the Urchin may clamber on the different levels of the base, which is nicely adapted for the mountaineering capacity of twenty-seven months. The low brick walls before the gymnasium and the University museum are also just right for an Urchin who has recently learned the fascination of walking on something raised above the ground, provided there is a curator near by to hold his hand. And then, as one walks away toward the South Street bridge an observant Urchin may spy the delightful spectacle of a freight train travelling apparently in midair. Some day, one hopes, all that fine tract of open space leading from the museum down to the railroad tracks may perhaps be beautified as a park or an addition to the University's quadrangle system. I don't know who owns it, but its architectural possibilities must surely make the city-planner's mouth water.

By this time the Urchin was beginning to feel a bit weary, and was glad of a lift on a parental shoulder. Then a Lombard Street car came along and took us up halfway across the bridge. So ended the Urchin's first introduction to a university education.

PINE STREET

Our neighbourhood is very genteel. I doubt if any one who has not lived in Philadelphia can imagine how genteel it is. Visitors from out of town are wont to sigh with rapture when they see our trim blocks of tall brick dwellings—that even cornice running in a smooth line for several hundred yards really is quite a sight—and exclaim, "Oh, I wish we had something like this in New York!" But our gentility is a little self-conscious, for we live on the very frontier of a region, darker in complexion, which is far from scrupulous in deportment. Uproarious and naïve are the humours of South Street, lying just behind us. Stanleys have gone exploring thither and come back with merry tales. South Street on a bright evening, its myriad barber shops gleaming with lathered dusky cheeks, wafting the essence of innumerable pomades and lotions, that were a Travel indeed. On South Street the veins of life run close to the surface.

We are no less human on our street, but it takes a bit more study to get at the secret. There is a certain reticence about us. It would take an earthquake to cause much fraternization along Pine Street. Perhaps it is because three houses out of every four bear the tablets of doctors. The average layman fears to stop and speak to his neighbour for fear it will develop into a professional matter. We board up our front windows at night with heavy wooden shutters. We have no druggists, only "apothecaries." These apothecaries are closed on Sundays. They sell stamps in little isinglass capsules, to be quite sanitary, two twos in a capsule for five cents. In their shops you can still get soda water with "plain cream" and shaved ice, such as was customary twenty-five years ago. When our doctors go away for the summer, someone comes twice a week from June to October to polish up the little silver name plate. It is the custom in our neighbourhood (so one observes through drawing room windows) to have reading lamps with rosy pink shades and at least two beautiful daughters of débutante age. I hope I am not unjust, but our street looks to me like the kind of place where people take warm baths, in a roomy old china tub, on Sunday afternoons. After that, they go downstairs and play a hymn on the piano, at twilight.

There are a number of very odd features about our neighbourhood. There is a large schoolhouse at the next corner, but as far as I can see, it is not used as a school, not for children, at any rate. Sometimes, about 8 o'clock in the evening, I see the building

71

gloriously illuminated, and a lonely lady stooped and assiduous at a table. She seems quite solitary. Perhaps her researches are so poignant that the school board has prescribed entire silence. But midway down the block is a very jolly little private school, to which very genteel children may be seen approaching early in the morning. The little girls come with a bustle of starch, on foot, accompanied by governesses; the small boys arrive in limousines. They are small boys dressed very much in the English manner, with heavy woollen stockings ending just below the knee. They probably do not realize that their tailor has carefully planned them to look like dear little English boys. Then there is a very mysterious small theatre near by. If it were a movie theatre, what a boon it would be! But no, it is devoted to a strange cult called the Religion of Business, which meets there on Sundays. Before that, there was a Korean congress there. There is a lovely green room in this theatre, but not much long green in the box office. Philadelphia prefers Al Jolson to Hank Ibsen.

We have our tincture of vie de Bohème, though, in our little French table d'hôte, a thoroughly atmospheric place. Delightful Madame B., with her racy philosophy of life, what delicious soups and salads she serves! Happy indeed are those who have learned the way to her little tables, and heard her cheerful cry "À la cuisine!" when one of her small dogs prowls into the dining room. Equally unique is the old curiosity shop near by, one of the few genuine "notion" shops left in the city (though there is a delightful one on Market Street near Seventeenth, to enter which is to step into a country village). This is just the kind of shop bought by the old gentleman in one of Frank Stockton's agreeable tales, "Mr. Tolman," in the volume called "The Magic Egg". The proprietress, charming and conversable lady, will sell you anything in the "notions" line, from a paper of pins to garter elastic. Then there is the laundry, whose patrons carry on a jovial game known as "Looking for Your Own." Every week, by some cheery habit of confusion, the lists are lost, and one hunts through shelves of neatly piled and crisply laundered garments to pick out one's own collars, pyjamas, or whatever it may be. The amusing humour of this pastime must be experienced to be understood.

The little cigar and magazine shop on the corner is the political and social focus of the neighbourhood. I shall never forget the pallid and ghastly countenance of the newsdealer when the rumour first went the rounds that "Hampy" was elected. Every evening a little gathering of local sages meets in the shop; on tilted chairs, in a haze of tobacco, they while the hours away. In tobacco the host adheres to the standard blends, but in literature he is enterprising. Until recently this was the only place I know in Philadelphia where one could get the Illustrated London News every week.

There are twinges of modernity going on along our street. Some of the old houses have been remodeled into apartments. There is an "electric shoe repairer" just round the corner. But the antique dealers and plumbers for which the street is famous still hold sway; the fine old brick pavement still collects rain water in its numerous dimpled hollows, and the yellowish marble horse-blocks adorn the curb. The nice shabby stables in the little side streets have not yet been turned into studios by artists, and the neighbourhood's youngest urchins set sail for Rittenhouse Square every morning on their fleet of "kiddie-cars." Their small stout legs, twinkling along the pavements in white gaiters on a wintry day, are a pleasant sight. Even our urchins are notably genteel. Surrounded on all sides by the medical profession, they are reared on registered milk and educator crackers. If Philadelphia ever betrays its soul, it does so on this delightful, bland, and genteel highway.

PERSHING IN PHILADELPHIA

The pavement in front of Independence Hall was a gorgeous jumble of colours. The great silken flags of the Allies, carried by vividly costumed ladies, burned and flapped in the wind. On a pedestal stood the Goddess of Liberty, in rich white draperies that seemed fortunately of sufficient texture to afford some warmth, for the air was cool. She graciously turned round for Walter Crail, the photographer of our contemporary, the Evening Public Ledger, to take a shot at her.

Down Chestnut Street came a rising tide of cheers. A squadron of mounted police galloped by. Then the First City Troop, with shining swords. Fred Eckersburg, the State House engineer, was fidgeting excitedly inside the hall, in a new uniform. This was Fred's greatest day, but we saw that he was worried about Martha Washington, the Independence Hall cat. He was apprehensive lest the excitement should give her a fit or a palsy. Independence Hall is no longer the quiet old place Martha used to enjoy before the war.

The Police Band struck up "Hail to the Chief." Yells and cheers burst upward from the ground like an explosion. Here he was, standing in the car. There was the famous chin, the Sam Browne belt, the high laced boots with spurs. Even the tan gloves carried in the left hand. There was the smile, without which no famous man is properly equipped for public life. There was Governor Sproul's placid smile, too, but the Mayor seemed too excited to smile. Rattle, rattle, rattle went the shutters of the photographers. Up the scarlet lane of carpet came the general. His manner has a charming, easy grace. He saluted each one of the fair ladies garbed in costumes of our Allies, but taking care not to linger too long in front of any one of them lest any embracing should get started. A pattering of tiger lilies or some such things came dropping down from above. He passed into the hall, which was cool and smelt like a wedding with a musk of flowers.

While the Big Chief was having a medal presented to him inside the hall we managed to scuttle round underneath the grand stand and take up a pencil of vantage just below the little pulpit where the general was to speak. Here the crowd groaned against a bulwark of stout policemen. Philadelphia cops, bless them, are the best tempered in the world. (How Boston must envy us.) Genially two

74

gigantic bluecoats made room against the straining hawser for young John Fisher, aged eleven, of 332 Greenwich Street. John is a small, freckle-faced urchin. It was amusing to see him thrusting his eager little beezer between the vast, soft, plushy flanks of two patrolmen. He had been there over two hours waiting for just this adventure. Then, to assert the equality of the sexes, Mildred Dubivitch, aged eleven, and Eva Ciplet, aged nine, managed to insert themselves between the chinks in the line of cops. An old lady more than eighty years old was sitting placidly in a small chair just inside the ropes. She had been in the square more than five hours, and the police had found her a seat. "Are you going to put Pershing's name in, too?" asked John as we noted his address.

Independence Square never knew a more thrilling fifteen minutes. The trees were tossing and bending in the thrilling blue air. There was a bronzy tint in their foliage, as though they were putting on olive drab in honour of the general. Great balloons of silver clouds scoured across the cobalt sky. At one minute to 11 Pershing appeared at the top of the stand. The whole square, massed with people, shook with cheers.

Had it been any other man we would have said the general was frightened. He came down the aisle of the stand with his delightful, easy, smiling swing; but he looked shrewdly about, with a narrow-eyed, puckered gaze. He was plainly a little flabbergasted. He seemed taken aback by the greatness of Philadelphia's voice. He said something to himself. On his lips it looked like "What the deuce," or something of similar purport. He sat down on a chair beside Governor Sproul. Not more than four feet away, amazed at our own audacity, we peered over the floor of the stand.

He was paler than we expected. He looked a bit tired. Speaking as a father, we were pleased to note the absence of Warren, who was (we hope) getting a good sleep somewhere. We had a good look at the renowned chin, which is well worth study. It must be a hard chin to shave. It juts upward, reaching a line exactly below the brim of his cap. Below his crescent moustache there is no lower lip visible: it is tucked and folded in by the rising thrust of the jaw. It is this which gives him the "grim" aspect which every reader of the papers hears about. He is grim, there's no doubt about it, with the grimness of a man going through a tough ordeal. "I can see him all right," squeaked little John Fisher, "but he doesn't see me." The first two rows of seats at the right of the aisle were crammed with generals, two-star and three-star. From our lowly station we could see a grand panorama of mahogany leather boots and the flaring curves of riding breeches. It was a great day for Sam Browne. The thought came to us that has reached us before. The higher you go in the A. E. F. the more the officers are tailored after the English manner. It is the finest proof of international cousinship. When England and America wear the same kind of clothes, alliance is knit solid.

Pershing sat with his palms on his knees. He looked worried. There was a wavering crease down his lean cheeks. The plumply genial countenance of Governor Sproul next to him was an odd contrast to that dry, hard face. The bell in the tower tolled eleven times. He stood up for the photographers. Walter Crail, appearing from somewhere, sprang up on the parapet facing the general. "Look this way!" he shouted as the general turned toward some movie men. That will be Walter's first cry when he gets to heaven, or wherever. Mayor Smith's face was pallid with excitement. His nicely draped trouserings, which were only six inches from our notebook, quivered slightly as he said fifteen words of introduction.

As Pershing stood up to speak the crowd surged forward. The general was worried. "Don't, don't! Somebody will get hurt!" he called sharply. Then Mayor Smith surged forward also and said something to the police about watching the crowd.

The general took off his cap. Holding it in his left hand (with the gloves) he patted his close-cropped hair nervously. He frowned. He began to speak.

The speech has already been covered by our hated rivals. We will not repeat it, save to say that it was as crisp, clean-cut, and pointed as his chin. He was nervous, as we could see by the clenching and unclenching of his hands. His voice is rather high. We liked him for not being a suave and polished speaker. He gestured briskly with a pointing forefinger, and pronounced the word patriotic with a short A—"pattriotic." Later he stumbled over it again and got it out as patterotism. We liked him again for that. He doesn't have to pronounce it, anyway. We liked him best of all for the unconscious slip he made. "This reception," he said, "I understand is for the splendid soldiery of America that played such an important part in the war with our Allies." A respectful ripple of laughter passed over the stand at this, but he did not notice it. He was fighting too hard to think what to say next. We liked him, too, for saying "such an important part." A man who had been further away from the fighting would have said that it was America, alone and unaided,

76

that won the war. He is just as we have hoped he would be: a plain, blunt man. We have heard that he is going to enter the banking business. We'd like to have an account at that bank.

FALL FEVER

About this time of year, when the mellow air swoons (as the poets say) with golden languor and the landscape is tinged a soft brown like a piece of toast, we feel the onset and soft impeachment of fall fever.

Fall fever is (in our case at any rate) more insidious than the familiar disease of spring. Spring fever impels us to get out in the country; to seize a knotted cudgel and a pouchful of tobacco and agitate our limbs over the landscape. But the drowsiness of autumn is a lethargy in the true sense of that word—a forgetfulness. A forgetfulness of past discontents and future joys; a forgetfulness of toil that is gone and leisure to come; a mere breathing existence in which one stands vacantly eyeing the human scene, living in a gentle simmer of the faculties like a boiling kettle when the gas is turned low.

Fall fever, one supposes, is our inheritance from the cave man, who (like the bear and the—well, some other animal, whatever it is) went into hibernation about the first of November. Autumn with its soft inertia lulled him to sleep. He ate a hearty meal, raked together some dry leaves, curled up and slid off until the alarm clock of April.

This agreeable disease does not last very long with the modern man. He fights bravely against it; then the frost comes along, or the coal bill, and stings him into activity. But for a few days its genial torpor may be seen (by the observant) even in our bustling modern career. When we read yesterday that Judge Audenried's court clerks had fallen asleep during ballot-counting proceedings we knew that the microbe was among us again. Keats, in his lovely Ode, describes the figure of Autumn as stretched out "on a half-reaped furrow sound asleep." Unhappily the conventions forbid city dwellers from curling up on the pavements for a cheerful nap. If one were brave enough to do so, unquestionably many would follow his example. But the urbanite has taught himself to doze upright. You may see many of us, standing dreamily before Chestnut Street show windows in the lunch hour, to all intents and purposes in a state of slumber. Yesterday, in that lucid shimmer of warmth and light, a group stood in front of a doughnut window near Ninth Street: not one of them was more than half awake. Similarly a gathering watched the three small birds who have become a traditional window ornament on

78

Chestnut Street (they have recently moved from an oculist to a correspondence course office) and a faint whisper of snoring arose on the sultry air. The customs of city life permit a man to stand still as long as he likes if he will only pretend to be watching something. We saw a substantial burgher pivoted by the window of Mr. Albert, the violin maker, on Ninth Street. Apparently he was studying the fine autographed photo of Patti there displayed; but when we sidled near we saw that his eyes were closed; this admirable person, who seemed to be what is known as a "busy executive," and whose desk undoubtedly carries a plate-glass sheet with the orisons of Swett Marden under it, was in a blissful doze.

Modern life (as we say) struggles against this sweet enchantment of autumn, but Nature is too strong for us. Why is it that all these strikes occur just at this time of year? The old hibernating instinct again, perhaps. The workman has a subconscious yearning to scratch together a nice soft heap of manila envelopes and lie down on that couch for a six months' ear-pounding. There are all sorts of excuses that one can make to one's self for waving farewell to toil. Only last Sunday we saw this ad in a paper:

> HEIRS WANTED. The war is over and has made many new heirs. You may be one of them. Investigate. Many now living in poverty are rich, but don't know it.

Now what could be simpler (we said to ourself as we stood contemplating those doughnuts) than to forsake our jolly old typewriter and spend a few months in "investigating" whether any one had made us his heir? It might be. Odd things have happened. Down in Washington Square, for instance (we thought), are a number of sun-warmed benches, very reposeful to the sedentary parts, on which we might recline and think over the possibility of our being rich unawares. We hastened thither, but apparently many had had the same idea. There was not a bench vacant. The same was true in Independence Square and in Franklin Square. We will never make a good loafer. There is too much competition.

So we came back, sadly, to our rolltop and fell to musing. We picked up a magazine and found some pictures showing how Mary Pickford washes her hair. "If I am sun-drying my hair," said Mary (under a photo showing her reclining in a lovely garden doing just that), "I usually have the opportunity to read a scenario or do some other duty which requires concentration." And it occurred to us that if a strain like that is put upon a weak woman we surely ought to be able to go on moiling for a while, Indian summer or not. And then we found some pictures by our favourite artist, Coles Phillips, with that lovely shimmer around the ankles, and we resolved to be strong and brave and have pointed finger-nails. But still, in the back of our mind, the debilitating influence of fall fever was at work. We said to ourself, without the slightest thought of printing it (for it seemed to put us in a false light), that the one triumphant and unanswerable epigram of mankind, the grandest and most resolute utterance in the face of implacable fate, is the snore.

TWO DAYS BEFORE CHRISTMAS

Will the hand-organ man please call? Our wife has dug up our old overcoat and insists on giving it to him. We intended to give it to the Honolulu Girls around at the Walnut Theatre, they looked a bit goose-fleshed last week, but we always have hay fever when we get near those grass skirts. Grass widows is what the profession calls the Hawaiian ladies. Hope the temperature isn't going up again. We love the old-fashioned Christmas and all that sort of thing. Nipping air makes cheeks pink; we love to see them nestled in fur coats on Chestnut Street. This is the time of year to do unexpected kindnesses. We know one man who stands in line for hours in front of movie theatres just in order to shout Merry Christmas through the little hole in the glass. Shaving seems less of a bore. Newspapers are supposed to be heartless, but they all take a hand in trying to help poor children. Find ourselves humming hymn tunes. Very odd, haven't been to a church for years. Great fun surprising people. We've been reading the new phone book; noticed several ways in which people might surprise each other by calling up and wishing many happy returns of the day. Why doesn't Beulah R. Wine ring up Mrs. Louis F. Beer, for instance? Or, A. D. Smoker and Burton J. Puffer might go around to W. C. Matchett, tobacconist, at 1635 South Second Street, and buy their Christmas cigars. George Wharton Pepper might give Mayme Salt a ring (on the phone, that is). What a pleasant voice that telephone operatrix has. Here's to you, child, and many of them. Grand time, Christmas.

Fine old Anglo-Saxon festival, Christmas. A time of jovial cheer and bracing mirth. Must be so, because Doctor Frank Crane and Ralph Waldo Trine have often said so. Christmas hard on people like that, however: they are bursting with the Christmas spirit all the year round; very trying when the real occasion comes. That's the beauty of having a peevish and surly disposition: when one softens up at Christmas everybody notices it and is pleased. Chaucer, fine old English poet, first English humorist, gave good picture of Christmas cheer more than five hundred years ago. Never quoted on Christmas cards, why not copy it here? Chaucer's spelling very like Ring Lardner's, but good sort just the same. Says he:

> And this was, as thise bookes me remembre,
> The colde, frosty sesoun of Decembre....
> The bittre frostes with the sleet and reyn
> Destroyed hath the grene in every yard;

Janus sit by the fyre with double beard,
And drynketh of his bugle horn the wyn;
Biforn hym stant brawn of the tusked swyn,
And "Nowel" crieth every lusty man.

Janus, god of doors, what we call nowadays a janitor. Had two faces so he could watch the front and back door at once and get a double tip at Christmas time. Also, that was why he wore a beard; too much trouble to shave. We don't cry Nowel any more; instead we petition the janitor to send up a little more steam. But what a jolly picture Chaucer gives of Christmas! Wine to drink (fine ruddy wine, as red as the holly berries), crackling flitch of pig to eat, and a merry cry of welcome sounding at the threshold as your friends come stamping in through the snow.

Grand time, Christmas! No one is really a Philadelphian until he has waited for a Pine Street car on a snowy night. Please have my seat, madam, there's plenty of room on the strap. Wonder why the pavement on Chestnut Street is the slipperiest in the world? Always fall down just in front of our bank; most embarrassing; hope the paying teller doesn't see us. Very annoying to lose our balance just there. Awfully nice little girl in there who balances the books. Has a kind heart. The countless gold of a merry heart, as William Blake said. She looks awfully downcast when our balance gets the way it is now. Hate to disappoint her. Won't have our book balanced again for a devil of a while. Even the most surly is full of smiles nowadays. Most of us when we fall on the pavement (did you ever try it on Chestnut between Sixth and Seventh on a slippery day?) curse the granolithic trust and wamble there groaning. But not nowadays. Make the best of things. Fine panorama of spats.

Association of ideas. Everybody wears silk stockings at Christmas time. Excessive geniality of the ad-writers. Uproarious good cheer. Makes one almost ashamed to notice the high price of everything. Radicals being deported. Why not deport Santa Claus, too? Very radical notion that, love your neighbour better than yourself. Easy to do; very few of us such dam fools as to love ourselves, but so often when you love your neighbour she doesn't return it. Nice little boxes they have at the ten-cent stores, all covered with poinsettia flowers, to put presents in. Wonder when poinsettia began to be used as a Christmas decoration and why? Everyone in ten-cent store calls them "poinsettias," but named after J. R. Poinsett. Encyclopedia very handy at times; makes a good Christmas present, one dollar down and a dollar a month for life. Nobody can tell the difference between real pearls and imitation; somebody ought to put the oysters wise. Save them a lot of trouble and anxiety. Don't know just what duvetyne is, but there seems to be a lot of it drunk nowadays. Hope that clockwork train for the Urchin will arrive soon; we were hoping to have three happy evenings playing with it before he sees it. Fine to have children; lots of fun playing with their presents. We are sure that life after death is really so, because children always kick the blankets off at night. Fine bit of symbolism that; put it in a sermon, unless Doctor Conwell gets there first.

Grand time, Christmas! We vowed to try to take down our weight this winter, and then they put sugar back on the menu, and doughnut shops spring up on every street, and Charles F. Jenkins sent us a big sack of Pocono buckwheat flour and we're eating a basketful of griddle cakes every morning for breakfast. Terrible to be a coward; we always turn on the hot water first in the shower bath, except the first morning we used it. The plumber got the indicator on the wrong way round, and when you turn to the place marked HOT it comes down like ice. Our idea of a really happy man is the fellow driving a wagonload of truck just in front of a trolley car, holding it back all the way downtown; when he hears the motorman clanging away he pretends he thinks it's the Christmas chimes and sings "Hark the Herald Angels."

Speaking of Herald Angels reminds us of a good story about James Gordon Bennett; we'll spring it one of these days when we're hard up for copy. Jack Frost must be a married man, did you see him try to cover up the show windows with his little traceries the other day when the shopping was at its height? There was a pert little hat in a window on Walnut Street we were very much afraid someone might see; the frost saved us. Don't forget to put Red Cross seals on your letters. Delightful to watch the faces on the streets at Christmas time. Everybody trying hard to be pleasant; sometimes rather a strain. Curious things faces—some of them seem almost human; queer to think that each belongs to someone and no chance to get rid of it; sorry we're not in the mirror industry; never thought of it before, but it ought to be profitable. Happier most of us, if mirrors never had been invented. Hope all our nice-natured clients will have the best kind of a time; forgive us for not answering letters; we are too disillusioned about ourself to make any resolutions to do better. We're going home now; on the way we'll think of a lot of nice things we might have said, write them down and use them to-morrow. Hope Dorothy Gish will get something nice in her stocking. Don't make the obvious retort. Grand time, Christmas!

IN WEST PHILADELPHIA

Climbing aboard car No. 13—ominously labelled "Mt. Moriah"—I voyaged toward West Philadelphia. It was a keen day, the first snow of winter had fallen, and sparkling gushes of chill swept inward every time the side doors opened. The conductor, who gets the full benefit of this ventilation, was feeling cynical, and seeing his blue hands I didn't blame him. Long lines of ladies, fumbling with their little bags and waiting for change, stepped off one by one into the windy eddies of the street corners. One came up to pay her fare ten blocks or so before her destination, and then retired to her seat again. This puzzled the conductor and he rebuked her. The argument grew busy. To the amazement of the passengers this richly dressed female brandished lusty epithets. "You Irish mick!" she said. (One would not have believed it possible if he had not heard it.) "That's what I am, and proud of it," said he. The shopping solstice is not all fur coats and pink cheeks. If you watch the conductors in the blizzard season, and see the slings and arrows they have to bear, you will coin a new maxim. The conductor is always right.

It is always entertaining to move for a little in a college atmosphere. I stopped at College Hall at the University and seriously contemplated slipping in to a lecture. The hallways were crowded with earnest youths of both sexes—I was a bit surprised at the number of co-eds, particularly the number with red hair— discussing the tribulations of their lot. "Think of it," said one man, "I'm a senior, and carrying twenty-three hours. Got a thesis to do, 20,000 words." On a bulletin board I observed the results of a "General Intelligence Exam." It appears that 1,770 students took part. They were listed by numbers, not by names. It was not stated what the perfect mark would have been; the highest grade attained was 159, by Mr. (or Miss?) 735. The lowest mark was 23. I saw that both 440 and 1124 got the mark of 149. If these gentlemen (or ladies) are eager to play off the tie, it would be a pleasure to arrange a deciding competition for them. The elaborate care with which the boys and girls ignore one another as they pass in the halls was highly delightful, and reminded me of exactly the same thing at Oxford. But I saw the possible beginning of true romance in the following notice on one of the boards:

WANTED: Names and addresses of ten nice American

84

university students who must remain in Philadelphia over Christmas, away from home, to be invited to a Christmas Eve party to help entertain some Bryn Mawr College girls in one of the nicest homes in a suburb of Philadelphia.

Certainly there is the stage set for a short story. Perhaps not such a short one, either.

Naturally I could not resist a visit to the library, where most of the readers seemed wholly absorbed, though one student was gaping forlornly over a volume of Tennyson. I found an intensely amusing book, "Who's Who in Japan," a copy of which would be a valuable standby to a newspaper paragrapher in his bad moments. For instance:

Sasaki, Tetsutaro: One of the highest taxpayers of Fukushima-ken, President of the Hongu Reeling Partnership, Director of the Dai Nippon Radium Water Co.; brewer, reeler; born Aug., 1860.

Sakurai, Ichisaku: Member of the Niigata City Council; Director of the Niigata Gas Co., Niigata Savings Bank. Born June, 1872, Studied Japanese and Chinese classics and arithmetic. At present also he connects with the Niigata Orphanage and various other philanthropic bodies. Was imprisoned by acting contrary to the act of explosive compound for seven years. Recreations: reading, Western wine.

Relying on my apparent similarity to the average undergrad, I plunged into the sancta of Houston Hall and bought a copy of the Punch Bowl. What that sprightly journal calls "A little group of Syria's thinkers" was shooting pool. The big fireplaces, like most fireplaces in American colleges, don't seem to be used. They don't even show any traces of ever having been used, a curious contrast to the always blazing hearths of English colleges. The latter, however, are more necessary, as in England there is usually no other source of warmth. A bitter skirmish of winds, carrying powdered snow dust, nipped round the gateways of the dormitories and Tait McKenzie's fine statue of Whitefield stood sharply outlined against a cold blue sky. I lunched at a varsity hash counter on Spruce Street and bought tobacco in a varsity drug store, where a New York tailor, over for the day, was cajoling students into buying his "snappy styles" in time for Christmas. There is no more interesting game than watching a lot of college men, trying to pick out those who may

85

be of some value to the community in future—the scientists, poets, and teachers of the next generation. The well-dressed youths one sees in the varsity drug stores are not generally of this type.

The Evans School of Dentistry at Fortieth and Spruce is a surprising place. Its grotesque gargoyles, showing (with true medieval humour) the sufferings of tooth patients, are the first thing one notices. Then one finds the museum, in which is housed Doctor Thomas W. Evans's collection of paintings and curios brought back from France. Unfortunately there seems to be no catalogue of the items, so that there is no way of knowing what interesting associations belong to them. But most surprising of all is to find the travelling carriage of the Empress Eugenie in which she fled from France in the fatal September days of 1870. She spent her last night in France at the home of Doctor Evans, and there is a spirited painting by Dupray showing her leaving his house the next morning, ushered into the carriage by the courtly doctor. The old black barouche, or whatever one calls it, seems in perfect condition still, with the empress's monogram on the door panel. Only the other day we read in the papers that the remarkable old lady (now in her ninety-fourth year) has been walking about Paris, revisiting well-known scenes. How it would surprise her to see her carriage again here in this University building in West Philadelphia. The whole museum is delightfully French in flavour; as soon as one enters one seems to step back into the curiously bizarre and tragic extravagance of the Second Empire.

One passes into the dignified and placid residence section of Spruce and Pine streets, with its distinctly academic air. Behind those quiet walls one suspects bookcases and studious professors and all the delightful passions of the mind. On Baltimore Avenue the wintry sun shone white and cold; in Clark Park, Charles Dickens wore a little cap of snow, and Little Nell looked more pathetic than ever. There is a breath of mystery about Baltimore Avenue. What does that large sign mean, in front of a house near Clark Park—THE EASTERN TRAVELLERS? Then one comes to the famous shop of S. F. Hiram, the Dodoneaean Shoemaker he calls himself. This wise coloured man has learned the advertising advantages of the unusual. His placard reads:

Originator of that famous Dobrupolyi System of repairing.

When one enters and asks to know more about this system, he points to another placard, which says:

It assumes the nature and character of an appellative noun, and carries the article The System.

His shop contains odd curios as well as the usual traffic of a cobbler. "The public loves to be hood-winked," he adds sagely.

HORACE TRAUBEL

We wait with particular interest to hear what Philadelphia will have to say about the passing of Horace Traubel. Traubel was the official echo of the Great Voice of Camden, and in his obituary one may discern the vivacity of the Whitman tradition. This is a matter of no small concern to the curators of the Whitman cult. The soul of Philadelphia cannot be kept alive by conventions and statistics alone. Such men as Traubel have helped.

There are two kinds of rebels. By their neckties you may know them. Walt Whitman was of the kind that wears no necktie at all. Then there is the lesser sort, of which Traubel was one—the rebel who wears a flowing black bow tie with long trailers. Elbert Hubbard wore one of these. It is a mild rebellion of which this is symbol. It often goes with shell spectacles.

We never knew Horace Traubel, though he was the man we most wanted to meet when we came to Philadelphia. We have heard men of all conditions speak of him with affection and respect. He was dedicated from boyhood to the Whitman cause. From Walt himself he caught the habit of talking about Walt, and he carried it on with as much gusto and happiness as Walt did. Only recently he said in his little magazine The Conservator:

When I was quite small I used to want to be a great man. But in my observations of the old man's better than great way of meeting the gifts as well as the reverses of fate I didn't want to be a great man. I only wanted to stay unannexed to any institution as he was. No college ever decorated him. For the best of reasons. No college could. He could decorate them.

So Traubel remained unannexed. He was fired from a bank because he happened to take issue in public with one of the bank's chief depositors. He floated about happily, surrounded by young Whitman disciples, carrying on his guerrilla for what his leader called the "peerless, passionate, good cause" of human democracy. His little magazine led a precarious life, supported by good friends. His protest against iniquities was an honest, good-humoured protest.

Horace Traubel will be remembered, as he wished to be remembered, as the biographer of Whitman. Whitman also, we may add, wished Traubel to be so remembered. In his careful record of the Camden sage's utterances and pulse-beats he approached (as nearly as any one) the devoted dignity of Boswell. We were about to say the self-effacing devotion of Boswell; but the beauty of biography is that the biographer cannot wholly delete himself from the book. One is always curious about the recording instrument. When we see a particularly fine photograph our first question is always, "What kind of camera was it taken with?"

It seems to us—speaking only by intuition, for we never knew him—that Traubel was a happy man. He was untouched by many of the harassing ambitions that make the lives of prosperous men miserable. He was touched in boyhood by one simple and overmastering motive—to carry on the Whitman message and spread it out for the younger world. Much of the dunnage of life he cast overboard. He was too good a Whitman disciple to estimate success in the customary terms. When he left his job in the bank he opened an account in the Walt Whitman philosophy—and he kept a healthy balance there to the end.

II

NEW YORK

THE ANATOMY OF MANHATTAN

She is the only city whose lovers live always in a mood of wonder and expectancy. There are others where one may sink peacefully, contentedly into the life of the town, affectionate and understanding of its ways. But she, the woman city, who is bold enough to say he understands her? The secret of her thrilling and inscrutable appeal has never been told. How could it be? She has always been so much greater than any one who has lived with her. (Shall we mention Walt Whitman as the only possible exception? O. Henry came very near to her, but did he not melodramatize her a little, sometimes cheapen her by his epigrammatic appraisal, fit her too neatly into his plot? Kipling seemed to see her only as the brutal, heedless wanton.) Truly the magic of her spell can never be exacted. She changes too rapidly, day by day. Realism, as they call it, can never catch the boundaries of her pearly beauty. She needs a mystic.

No city so challenges and debilitates the imagination. Here, where wonder is a daily companion, desire to tell her our ecstasy becomes at last only a faint pain in the mind. If you would mute a poet's lyre, put him on a ferry from Jersey City some silver April morning; or send him aboard at Liberty Street in an October dusk. Poor soul, his mind will buzz (for years to come) after adequate speech to tell those cliffs and scarps, amethyst and lilac in the mingled light; the clear topaz chequer of window panes; the dull bluish olive of the river, streaked and crinkled with the churn of the screw! Many a poet has come to her in the wooing passion. Give him six months, he is merely her Platonist. He lives content with placid companionship. Where are his adjectives, his verbs? That inward knot of amazement, what speech can unravel it?

Her air, when it is typical, is light, dry, cool. It is pale, it is faintly tinctured with pearl and opal. Heaven is unbelievably remote; the

90

city itself daring so high, heaven lifts in a cautious remove. Light and shadow are fantastically banded, striped, and patchworked among her cavern streets; a cool, deep gloom is cut across with fierce jags and blinks of brightness. She smiles upon man who takes his ease in her colossal companionship. Her clean soaring perpendiculars call the eye upward. One wanders as a botanist in a tropical forest. That great smooth groinery of the Pennsylvania Station train shed: is it not the arching fronds of iron palm trees? Oh, to be a botanist of this vivid jungle, spread all about one, anatomist of the ribs and veins that run from the great backbone of Broadway!

To love her, one thinks, is to love one's fellows; each of them having some unknown share in her loveliness. Any one of her streets would be the study and delight of a lifetime. To speak at random, we think of that little world of brightness and sound bourgeois cheer that spreads around the homely Verdi statue at Seventy-third Street. We have a faithful affection for that neighbourhood, for reasons of our own. Within a radius, thereabouts, of a quarter-mile each way, we could live a year and learn new matters every day. They call us a hustling folk. Observe the tranquil afternoon light in those brownstone byways. Pass along leisurely Amsterdam Avenue, the region of small and genial shops, Amsterdam Avenue of the many laundries. See the children trooping upstairs to their own room at the St. Agnes branch of the Public Library. See the taxi drivers, sitting in their cars alongside the Verdi grass plot (a rural breath of new-mown turf sweetening the warm, crisp air) and smoking pipes. Every one of them is to us as fascinating as a detective story. What a hand they have had in ten thousand romances. At this very moment, what quaint and many-stranded destinies may hail them and drive off? But there they sit, placid enough, with a pipe and the afternoon paper. The light, fluttering dresses of enigmatic fair ones pass gayly on the pavement. Traffic flows, divides, and flows on, a sparkling river. Here is that mystery, a human being, buying a cigar. Here is another mystery asking for a glass of frosted chocolate. Why is it that we cannot accost that tempting riddle and ask him to give us an accurate précis of his life to date? And that red-haired burly sage, he who used to bake the bran muffins in the little lunchroom near by, and who lent us his Robby Burns one night—what has become of him?

So she teases us, so she allures. Sometimes, on the L, as one passes along that winding channel where the walls and windows come so close, there is a felicitous sense of being immersed, surrounded,

91

drowned in a great, generous ocean of humanity. It is a fine feeling. All life presses around one, the throb and the problem are close, are close. Who could be weary, who could be at odds with life, in such an embrace of destiny? The great tall sides of buildings fly open, the human hive is there, beautiful and arduous beyond belief. Here is our worship and here our lasting joy, here is our immortality of encouragement. Yes, perhaps O. Henry did say the secret after all: "He saw no longer a rabble, but his brothers seeking the ideal."

VESEY STREET

The first duty of the conscientious explorer is to study his own neighbourhood, so we set off to familiarize ourself with Vesey Street. This amiable byway (perhaps on account of the proximity of Washington Market) bases its culture on a solid appreciation of the virtue of good food, an admirable trait in any street. Upon this firm foundation it erects a seemly interest in letters. The wanderer who passes up the short channel of our street, from the docks to St. Paul's churchyard, must not be misled by the character of the books the bibliothecaries display in their windows. Outwardly they lure the public by Bob Ingersoll's lectures, Napoleon's Dream Book, efficiency encyclopædias and those odd and highly coloured small brochures of smoking-car tales of the Slow Train Through Arkansaw type. But once you penetrate, you may find quarry of a more stimulating kind. For fifteen cents we eloped with a first edition of Bunner's "Love in Old Cloathes," which we were glad to have in memory of the "old red box on Vesey Street" which Banner immortalized in rhyme, and which still stands (is it the same box?) by the railing of St. Paul's. Also, even nobler treasure to our way of thinking, did we not just now find (for fifteen cents) Hilaire Belloc's "Hills and the Sea," that enchanting little volume of essays, which we are almost afraid to read again. Belloc, the rogue—the devil is in him. Such a lusty beguilery moves in his nimble prose that after reading him it is hard not to fall into a clumsy imitation of his lively and frolic manner. There is at least one essayist in this city who fell subject to the hilarious Hilaire years ago. It is an old jape but not such a bad one: our friend Murray Hill will never return to the status quo ante Belloc.

But we were speaking of Vesey Street. It looks down to the water, and the soft music of steamship whistles comes tuning on a cold, gusty air. Thoroughly mundane little street, yet not unmindful of matters spiritual, bounded as it is by divine Providence at one end (St. Paul's) and by Providence, R. I. (the Providence Line pier) at the other. Perhaps it is the presence of the graveyard that has startled Vesey Street into a curious reversal of custom. On most other streets, we think, the numbers of the houses run even on the south side, odd on the north. But just the opposite on Vesey. You will find all even numbers on the north, odd on the south. Still, Wall Street errs in the same way.

If marooned or quarantined on Vesey Street a man might lead a life

93

of gayety and sound nourishment for a considerable while, without having recourse to more exalted thoroughfares. There are lodging houses in that row of old buildings down toward the docks; from the garret windows he could see masts moving on the river. For food he would live high indeed. Where will one see such huge glossy blue-black grapes; such enormous Indian River grapefruit; such noble display of fish—scallops, herrings, smelts, and the larger kind with their dead and desolate eyes? There are pathetic rows of rabbits, frozen stiff in the bitter cold wind; huge white hares hanging in rows; a tray of pigeons with their iridescent throat feathers catching gleams of the pale sunlight. There are great sacks of nuts, barrels of cranberries, kegs of olive oil, thick slabs of yellow cheese. On such a cold day it was pleasant to see a sign "Peanut Roasters and Warmers."

Passing the gloomy vista of Greenwich Street—under the "L" is one of those mysterious little vents in the floor of the street from which issues a continual spout of steam—our Vesey grows more intellectual. The first thing one sees, going easterly, is a sign: The Truth Seeker, One flight Up. The temptation is almost irresistible, but then Truth is always one flight higher up, so one reflects, what's the use? In this block, while there is still much doing in the way of food—and even food in the live state, a window full of entertaining chicks and ducklings clustered round a colony brooder—another of Vesey Street's interests begins to show itself. Tools. Every kind of tool that gladdens the heart of man is displayed in various shops. One realizes more and more that this is a man's street, and indeed (except at the meat market) few of the gayer sex are to be seen along its pavements. One of the tool shops has open-air boxes with all manner of miscellaneous oddments, from mouse traps to oil cans, and you may see delighted enthusiasts poring over the assortment with the same professional delight that ladies show at a notion counter. One of the tool merchants, however, seems to have weakened in his love of city existence, for he has put up a placard:

> *Wanted To Rent*
> *Small Farm*
> *Must Have Fruit and Spring Water*

How many years of repressed yearning may speak behind that modest ambition!

Our own taste for amusement leads us (once luncheon dispatched; you should taste Vesey Street's lentil soup) to the second-hand bookshops. Our imagined castaway, condemned to live on Vesey

Street for a term of months, would never need to languish for mental stimulation. Were he devout, there is always St. Paul's, as we have said; and were he atheist, what a collection of Bob Ingersoll's essays greets the faring eye! There is the customary number of copies of "The Pentecost of Calamity"; it seems to the frequenter of second-hand bazaars as though almost everybody who bought that lively booklet in the early days of the war must have sold it again since the armistice. Much rarer, we saw a copy of "Hopkins's Pond," that little volume of agreeable sketches written so long ago by Dr. Robert T. Morris, the well-known surgeon, and if we had not already a copy which the doctor inscribed for us we would certainly have rescued it from this strange exile.

There are only two of the really necessary delights of life that the Vesey Street maroon would miss. There is no movie, there are no doughnuts. We are wondering whether in any part of this city there has sprung up the great doughnut craze that has ravaged Philadelphia in the past months. As soon as prohibition became a certainty, certain astute merchants of the Quaker City devoted themselves to inoculating the public with a taste for these humble fritters, and now they bubble gayly in the windows of Philadelphia's most aristocratic thoroughfare. It is really a startling sight to see Philadelphia lining up for its noonday quota of doughnuts, and the merchants over there have devised an ingenious method of tempting the crowd. A funnel, erected over the frying sinkers, carries the fragrant fumes out through a transom and gushes it into the open air, so that the sniff of doughnuts is perceptible all down the block. There is a fortune waiting on Vesey Street for the man who will establish a doughnut foundry, and we solemnly pledge our own appetite and that of all our friends toward his success.[2]

At its upper end, perhaps in memory of the vanished Astor House, Vesey Street stirs itself into a certain magnificence, devoting its window space to jewellery and silver-mounted books of prayer. At this window one may regulate his watch at a clock warranted by Charles Frodsham of 84, Strand, to whose solid British accuracy we hereby pay decent tribute. Over all this varied scene lifts the shining javelin-head of the Woolworth Building, seen now and then in an almost disbelieved glimpse of sublimity; and the golden Lightning of the Telephone and Telegraph pinnacle, waving his zigzag brands in the sun.

---

[2] Since this was written, the lack has been supplied—on Park Row, just above the top of Vesey Street; probably the most luxurious doughnut shop ever conceived.

BROOKLYN BRIDGE

A windy day, one would have said in the dark channels of downtown ways. In the chop house on John Street, lunch-time patrons came blustering in, wrapped in overcoats and mufflers, with something of that air of ostentatious hardiness that men always assume on coming into a warm room from a cold street. Thick chops were hissing on the rosy grill at the foot of the stairs. In one of the little crowded stalls a man sat with a glass of milk. It was the first time we had been in that chop house for several years ... it doesn't seem the same. As Mr. Wordsworth said, it is not now as it hath been of yore. But still,

> The homely Nurse doth all she can
> To make her foster-child, her Inn-mate Man,
> Forget the glories he hath known.

It's a queer thing that all these imitation beers taste to us exactly as real beer did the first time we tasted it (we were seven years old) and shuddered. "Two glasses of cider," we said to the comely serving maid. Alas

> That nature yet remembers
> What was so fugitive.

There is a nice point of etiquette involved in lunching in a crowded chop house. Does the fact of having bought and eaten a moderate meal entitle one to sit with one's companion for a placid talk and smoke afterward? Or is one compelled to relinquish the table as soon as one is finished, to make place for later comers? These last are standing menacingly near by, gazing bitterly upon us as we look over the card and debate the desirability of having some tapioca pudding. But our presiding Juno has already settled the matter, and made courtesy a matter of necessity. "These gentlemen will be through in a moment," she says to the new candidates. Our companion, the amiable G–– W––, was just then telling us of a brand of synthetic whiskey now being distilled by a famous tavern of the underworld. The superlative charm of this beverage seems to be the extreme rigidity it imparts to the persevering communicant. "What does it taste like?" we asked. "Rather like gnawing furniture," said G–– W––. "It's like a long, healthy draught of shellac. It seems to me that it would be less trouble if you offered the barkeep fifty cents to hit you over the head with a hammer. The general effect would be about the same, and you wouldn't feel nearly so bad in the morning."

A windy day, and perishing chill, we thought as we strolled through the gloomy caverns and crypts underneath the Brooklyn Bridge. Those twisted vistas seen through the archways give an impression of wrecked Louvain. A great bonfire was burning in the middle of the street. Under the Pearl Street elevated the sunlight drifted through the girders in a lively chequer, patterning piles of gray-black snow with a criss-cross of brightness. We had wanted to show our visitor Franklin Square, which he, as a man of letters, had always thought of as a trimly gardened plot surrounded by quiet little old-fashioned houses with brass knockers, and famous authors tripping in and out. As we stood examining the façade of Harper and Brothers, our friend grew nervous. He was carrying under his arm the dummy of an "export catalogue" for a big brass foundry, that being his line of work. "They'll think we're free verse poets trying to get up courage enough to go in and submit a manuscript," he said, and dragged us away.

A windy day, we had said in the grimy recesses of Cliff and Dover streets. (Approaching this sentiment for the third time, perhaps we may be permitted to accomplish our thought and say what we had in mind.) But up on the airy decking of the Brooklyn Bridge, where we repaired with G—— W—— for a brief stroll, the afternoon seemed mild and tranquil. It is a mistake to assume that the open spaces are the windier. The subway is New York's home of Æolus, and most of the gusts that buffet us on the streets are merely hastening round a corner in search of the nearest subway entrance so that they can get down there where they feel they belong. Up on the bridge it was plain to perceive that the March sunshine had elements of strength. The air was crisp but genial. A few pedestrians were walking resolutely toward the transpontine borough; the cop on duty stood outside his little cabin with the air of one ungrieved by care. Behind us stood the high profiles of the lower city, sharpened against the splendidly clear blue sky which is New York's special blessing. On the water moved a large tug, towing barges. Smoke trailed behind it in the same easy and comfortable way that tobacco reek gushes over a man's shoulder when he walks across a room puffing his pipe.

The bridge is a curiously delightful place to watch the city from. Walking toward the central towers seems like entering a vast spider's web. The footway between the criss-cross cables draws one inward with a queer fascination, the perspective diminishing the network to the eye so that it seems to tighten round you as you advance. Even when there is but little traffic the bridge is never still. It is alive, trembling, vibrant, the foot moves with a springy recoil. One feels the lift and strain of gigantic forces, and looks in amazement on the huge sagging hawsers that carry the load. The bars and rods quiver, the whole lively fabric is full of a tremor, but one that conveys no sense of insecureness. It trembles as a tree whispers in a light air.

And of the view from the bridge, it is too sweeping to carry wholly in mind. Best, one thinks, it is seen in a winter dusk, when the panes of Manhattan's mountains are still blazing against a crystal blue-green sky, and the last flush of an orange sunset lingers in the west. Such we saw it once, coming over from Brooklyn, very hungry after walking in most of the way from Jamaica, and pledged in our own resolve not to break fast until reaching a certain inn on Pearl Street where they used to serve banana omelets. Dusk simplifies the prospect, washes away the lesser units, fills in the foreground with obliterating shadow, leaves only the monstrous sierras of Broadway jagged against the vault. It deepens this incredible panorama into broad sweeps of gold and black and peacock blue which one may file away in memory, tangled eyries of shining windows swimming in empty air. As seen in the full brilliance of noonday the bristle of detail is too bewildering to carry in one clutch of the senses. The eye is distracted by the abysses between buildings, by the uneven elevation of the summits, by the jumbled compression of the streets. In the vastness of the scene one looks in vain for some guiding principle of arrangement by which vision can focus itself. It is better not to study this strange and disturbing outlook too minutely, lest one lose what knowledge of it one has. Let one do as the veteran prowlers of the bridge: stroll pensively to and fro in the sun, taking man's miracles for granted, exhilarated and content.

THREE HOURS FOR LUNCH

Hudson Street has a pleasant savour of food. It resounds with the dull rumble of cruising drays, which bear the names of well-known brands of groceries; it is faintly salted by an aroma of the docks. One sees great signs announcing cocoanut and whalebone or such unusual wares; there is a fine tang of coffee in the air round about the corner of Beach Street. Here is that vast, massy brick edifice, the New York Central freight station, built 1868, which gives an impression of being about to be torn down. From a dilapidated upper window hangs a faded banner of the Irish Republic. At noontime this region shows a mood of repose. Truckmen loll in sunny corners, puffing pipes, with their curved freight hooks hung round their necks. In a dark smithy half a dozen sit comfortably round a huge wheel which rests on an anvil, using it as a lunch table. Near Canal Street two men are loading ice into a yellow refrigerator car, and their practiced motions are pleasant to watch. One stands in the wagon and swings the big blocks upward with his tongs. The other, on the wagon roof, seizes the piece deftly and drops it through a trap on top of the car. The blocks of ice flash and shimmer as they pass through the sunshine. In Jim O'Dea's blacksmith shop, near Broome Street, fat white horses are waiting patiently to be shod, while a pink glow wavers outward from the forge.

At the corner of Hudson and Broome streets we fell in with our friend Endymion, it being our purpose to point out to him the house, one of that block of old red dwellings between Hudson and Varick, which Robert C. Holliday has described in "Broome Street Straws," a book which we hope is known to all lovers of New York local colour. Books which have a strong sense of place, and are born out of particular streets—and especially streets of an odd, rich, and well-worn flavour—are not any too frequent. Mr. Holliday's Gissingesque appreciation of the humours of landladies and all the queer fish that shoal through the backwaters of New York lodging houses makes this Broome Street neighbourhood exceedingly pleasant for the pilgrim to examine. It was in Mr. Holliday's honour that we sallied into a Hudson Street haberdashery, just opposite the channel of Broome Street, and adorned ourself with a new soft collar, also having the pleasure of seeing Endymion regretfully wave away some gorgeous mauve and pink neckwear that the agreeable dealer laid before him with words of encouragement. We also stood tranced by a marvellous lithograph advertising a roach powder in a neighbouring window, and wondered whether Mr. Holliday himself could have drawn the original in the days when he and Walter Jack Duncan lived in garrets on Broome Street and were art students together. Certainly this picture had the vigorous and spirited touch that one would expect from the draughting wrist of Mr. Holliday. It showed a very terrible scene, apparently a civil war among the roaches, for one army of these agile insects was treasonously squirting a house with the commended specific, and the horrified and stricken inmates were streaming forth and being carried away in roach ambulances, attended by roach nurses, to a neighbouring roach cemetery. All done on a large and telling scale, with every circumstance of dismay and reproach on the faces of the dying blattidæ. Not even our candour, which is immense, permits us to reprint the slogan the manufacturer has adopted for his poster: those who go prowling on Hudson Street may see it for themselves.

In the old oyster and chop house just below Canal Street we enjoyed a very agreeable lunch. To this place the Broome Street garreteers (so Mr. Holliday has told us) used to come on days of high prosperity when some cheque arrived from a publisher. At that time the tavern kept an open fireplace, with a bright nest of coals in the chilly season; and there was a fine mahogany bar. But we are no laudator of acted time; the fireplace has been bricked up, it is true; but the sweet cider is admirable, and as for the cheesecake, we would back it against all the Times Square variety that Ben De Casseres rattles about. It is delightful and surprising to find on Hudson Street an ordinary so droll and Dickensish in atmosphere, and next door is a window bearing the sign Walter Peter. We feel sure that Mr. Holliday, were he still living in those parts, would have cajoled the owner into changing that E to an A.

Our stroll led us north as far as Charlton Street, which the geographers of Greenwich Village claim as the lower outpost of their domain. Certainly it is a pleasing byway, running quietly through the afternoon, and one lays an envious eye upon the demure brick houses, with their old-fashioned doorways, pale blue shutters, and the studio windows on the southern side. At the corner of Varick Street is a large house showing the sign, "Christopher Columbus University of America." Macdougal Street gives one a distant blink of the thin greenery of Washington Square.

An unexpected impulse led us eastward on Grand Street, to revisit Max Maisel's interesting bookshop.—We had never forgotten the thrill of finding this place by chance one night when prowling toward Seward Park. In bookshops of a liberal sort we always find it advisable to ask first of all for a copy of Frank Harris's "The Man Shakespeare." It is hardly ever to be found (unfortunately), so the inquiry is comparatively safe for one in a frugal mood; and it is a tactful question, for the mention of this book shows the bookseller that you are an intelligent and understanding kind of person, and puts intercourse on good terms at once. However, we did find one book that we felt we simply had to have, as it is our favourite book for giving away to right-minded people—"The Invisible Playmate," by William Canton. We fear that there are still lovers of children who do not know this book; but if so, it is not our fault.

Grand Street is a child at heart, and one may watch it making merry not only along the pavement but in the shop windows. Endymion's gallant spirit was strongly uplifted by this lively thoroughfare, and he strode like one whose heart was hitting on all six cylinders. Max Maisel's bookshop alone is enough to put one in a seemly humour. But then one sees the gorgeous pink and green allurements of the pastry cooks' windows, and who can resist those little lemon-flavoured, saffron-coloured cakes, which are so thirst-compelling and send one hastily to the nearest bar for another beaker of cider? And it seems natural to find here the oldest toyshop in New York, where Endymion dashed to the upper floor in search of juvenile baubles, and we both greatly admired the tall, dark, and beauteous damsel who waited on us with such patience and charity. Endymion by this time was convinced that he was living in the very heart and climax of a poem; he became more and more unreal as we walked along: we could see his physical outline (tenuous enough at best) shimmer and blur as he became increasingly alcaic.

Along the warm crowded pavement there suddenly piped a liquid, gurgling, chirring whistle, rising and dropping with just the musical trill that floats from clumps of creekside willows at this time of year. We had passed several birdshops on our walk, and supposed that another was near. A song sparrow, was our instant conclusion, and we halted to see where the cage could be hung. And then we saw our warbler. He was little and plump and red-faced, with a greasy hat and a drooping beer-gilded moustache, and he wore on his coat a bright blue peddler's license badge. He shuffled along, stooping over a pouch of tin whistles and gurgling in one as he went. There's your poem, we said to Endymion—"The Song-Sparrow on Grand Street."

We propose to compile a little handbook for truants, which we shall call "How to Spend Three Hours at Lunch Time." This idea occurred to us on looking at our watch when we got back to our kennel.

PASSAGE FROM SOME MEMOIRS

How long ago it seems, that spring noonshine when two young men (we will call them Dactyl and Spondee) set off to plunder the golden bag of Time. These creatures had an oppressive sense that first Youth was already fled. For one of them, in fact, it was positively his thirtieth birthday; poor soul, how decrepitly he flitted in front of motor trucks. As for the other, he was far decumbent in years, quite of a previous generation, a perfect Rameses, whose senile face was wont to crack into wrinklish mirth when his palsied cronies called him the greatest poet born on February 2, 1886.

It was a day—well, it is fortunate that some things do not have to be described. Suppose one had to explain to the pallid people of the thither moon what a noonday sunshine is like in New York about the Nones of May? It could not be done to carry credence. Let it be said it was a Day, and leave it so. You have all known that gilded envelopment of sunshine and dainty air.

These pitiful creatures arose from the subway at Fourteenth Street and took the world in their right hands. From this revolving orb, said they, they would squeeze a luncheon hour of exquisite satisfactions. They gazed sombrely at Union Square, and uttered curious reminiscences of the venerable days when one of them had worked, actually toiled for a living, upon the shores of that expanse. Ten years had passed (yes, at least ten—O edax rerum!). Upon a wall these observant strollers saw a tablet to the memory of William Lloyd Garrison. Strange, said they, we never noticed this before. Ah, said one, this is hallowed ground. It was near here that I used to borrow a quarter, the day before pay-day, to buy my lunch. The other contributed similar recollections. And now, quoth he, I am grown so prosperous that when I need money I can't afford to borrow less than two hundred dollars.

They lunched (one brushes away the mist of time to recall the details) where the bright sunlight fell athwart a tablecloth of excellent whiteness. They ate (may one be precise at so great a distance?)—yes, they ate broiled mackerel to begin with; the kind of mackerel called (but why?) Spanish. Whereupon succeeded a course of honeycomb tripe, which moved Dactyl to quoting Rabelais, something that Grangousier had said about tripes. Only by these tripes is memory supported and made positive, for it was the first time either had tackled this dish. Concurrent with the tripes, one inducted the other into the true mystery of blending shandygaff, explaining the first doctrine of that worthy draught, which is that the beer must be poured into the beaker before the ginger ale, for so arises a fatter and lustier bubblement of foam. The reason whereof they leave no testament. While this portion of the meal was under discussion their minds moved free, unpinioned, with airy lightness, over all manner of topics. It seemed no effort at all to talk. Ripe, mellow with long experience of men and matters, their comments were notable for wisdom and sagacity. The waiter, overhearing shreds of their discourse, made a private notation to the effect that these were Men of Large Affairs. Then they embarked upon some salty crackers, enlivened with Camembert cheese and green-gage jam. By this time they were touching upon religion, from which they moved lightly to the poems of Louise Imogen Guiney. It is all quite distinct as one looks back upon it.

Issuing upon the street, Dactyl said something about going back to the office, but the air and sunlight said him nay. Rather, remarked Spondee, let us fare forward upon this street and see what happens. This is ever a comely doctrine, adds the chronicler. They moved gently, not without a lilac trailing of tobacco fume, across quiet stretches of pavement. In the blue upwardness stood the tower of the Metropolitan Life Building, a reminder that humanity as a whole pays its premiums with decent regularity. They conned the nice gradations of tint in the spring foliage of Gramercy Park. They talked, a little soberly, of thrift, and of their misspent years.

Lexington Avenue lay guileless beneath their rambling footfalls. At the corner of Twenty-second Street was a crowd gathered, and a man with the customary reverted cap in charge of a moving picture machine. A swift car drew up before the large house at the southeast corner. Thrill upon thrill: something being filmed for the movies! In the car, a handsome young rogue at the wheel, and who was this blithe creature in shiny leather coat and leather cap, with crumpling dark curls cascading beneath it? A suspicion tinkled in the breast of Spondee, in those days a valiant movie fan. Up got the young man, and hopped out of the car. Up stood the blithe creature—how neatly breeched, indeed, a heavenly forked radish—and those shining riding boots! She dismounted—lifted down (so unnecessarily it seemed) by the rogue. She stood there a moment and Spondee was convinced. Dorothy Gish, said he to Dactyl. Miss Gish and her escort darted into the house, the camera man reeling busily. At an upper window of the dwelling a white-haired lady was looking out,

103

between lace curtains, with a sort of horror. Query, was she part of the picture, or only the aristocratic owner of the house, dismayed at finding her home suddenly become part of a celluloid drama? Spondee had always had a soft spot in his heart for Miss Dorothy, esteeming her a highly entertaining creature. He was disappointed in the tranquil outcome of the scene. He had hoped to see leaping from windows and all manner of hot stuff. Near by stood a coloured groom with a horse. The observers concluded that Miss Gish was to do a little galloping shortly. Dactyl and Spondee moved away. Spondee quoted a poem he had once written about Miss Dorothy. He recollected only two lines:

She makes all the rest seem a shoal of poor fish
So we cast our ballot for Dorothy Gish.

Peering again into the dark backward and abysm, it seems that the two rejuvenated gossips trundled up on Lexington Avenue to Alfred Goldsmith's cheerful bookshop. Here they were startled to hear Mr. Goldsmith cry: "Well, Chris, here are some nice bones for you." One of these visitors assumed this friendly greeting was for him, but then it was explained that Mr. Goldsmith's dog, named Christmas, was feeling seedy, and was to be pampered. At this moment in came the postman with a package of books, arrived all the way from Canada. One of these books was "Salt of the Sea," a volume of tales by Morley Roberts, and upon this Spondee fell with a loud cry, for it contained "The Promotion of the Admiral," being to his mind a tale of great virtue which he had not seen in several years. Dactyl, meanwhile, was digging out some volumes of Gissing, and on the faces of both these creatures might have been seen a pleasant radiation of innocent cheer. Mr. Goldsmith also exhibited (it is still remembered) a beautiful photo of Walt Whitman, which entertained the visitors, for it showed old Walt with his coat-sleeve full of pins, which was ever Walt's way.

How long ago it all seems. Does Miss Dorothy still act for the pictures? Does Chris, the amiable Scots terrier, still enjoy his bones? Does old Dactyl still totter about his daily tasks? Queer to think that it happened only yesterday. Well, time runs swift in New York.

FIRST LESSONS IN CLOWNING

A medley of crashing music, pungently odd and exhilarating smells, the roaring croon of the steam calliope, the sweet lingering savour of clown-white grease paint, elephants, sleek barking seals, trained pigs, superb white horses, frolicking dogs, exquisite ladies in tights and spangles, the pallid Venuses of the "living statuary," a whole jumble of incongruous and fantastic glimpses, moving in perfect order through its arranged cycles—this is the blurred and ecstatic recollection of an amateur clown at the circus.

It was pay day that afternoon and all the performers were in cheerful humour. Perhaps that was why the two outsiders, who played a very inconspicuous part in the vast show, were so gently treated. Certainly they had approached the Garden in some secret trepidation. They had had visions of dire jests and grievous humiliations: of finding themselves suddenly astride the bare backs of berserk mules, or hoisted by blazing petards, or douched with mysterious cascades of icy water. Pat Valdo had written: "I am glad to hear you are going to clown a bit. I hope you both will enjoy the experience." To our overwrought imaginations this sounded a little ominous. What would Pat and his lively confrères do to us?

We need not have feared. Not in the most genial club could we have been more kindly treated than in the dressing room where we found Pat Valdo opening his trunk and getting out the antic costumes he had provided. (The eye of a certain elephant, to tell the truth, was the only real embarrassment we suffered. We happened to stand by him as he was waiting to go on, and in his shrewd and critical orb we saw a complete disdain. He spotted us at once. He knew us for interlopers. He knew that we were not a real clown, and his eye showed a spark of scorn. We felt shamed, and slunk away.)

A liberal coating of clown-white, well rubbed into the palms before applying; a rich powdering of talcum; and decorations applied by Pat Valdo with his red and black paint-sticks—these give an effect that startles the amateur when he considers himself in the mirror. Topped with a skull-cap of white flannel (on which perches a supreme oddity in the way of a Hooligan hat) and enveloped in a baggy Pierrot garment—one is ready to look about and study the dressing room, where our fellows, in every kind of gorgeous grotesquerie, are preparing for the Grand Introductory Pageant—

105

followed by the "Strange People." (They don't call them Freaks any more.) Here is Johannes Joseffson, the Icelandic Gladiator, sitting on his trunk, with his bare feet gingerly placed on his slippers to keep them off the dusty floor while he puts on his wrestling tights. As he bends over with arched back, and raises one leg to insert it into the long pink stocking, one must admire the perfect muscular grace of his thighs and shoulders. Here is the equally muscular dwarf, being massaged by a friend before he dons his pink frills and dashing plumed hat and becomes Mlle. Spangletti, "the marvel equestrienne, darling of the Parisian boulevards." Here is the inevitable Charley Chaplin, and here the dean of all the clowns, an old gentleman of seventy-four, in his frolicsome costume, as lively as ever. Here is a trunk inscribed Australian Woodchoppers, and sitting on it one of the woodchoppers himself, a quiet, humorous, cultivated gentleman with a great fund of philosophy. A rumour goes the rounds—as it does behind the scenes in every kind of show. "Do you know who we have with us to-day? I see one of the boxes is all decorated up." "It's Mrs. Vincent Astor." "Who's she?" interjects the Australian woodchopper, satirically. "It's General Wood." "Did you hear, Wood and Pershing are here to-day?" Charley Chaplin asserts that he has "a good gag" that he's going to try out to-day and see how it goes. One of the other clowns in the course of dressing comes up to Pat Valdo, and Pat introduces his two pupils. "Newspaper men, hey?" says the latter. "What did you tell me for? I usually double-cross the newspaper men when they come up to do some clowning," he explains to us. We are left wondering in what this double-crossing consists. Suddenly they all troop off down the dark narrow stairs for the triumphal entry. The splendour of this parade may not be marred by any clown costumes, so the two novices are left upstairs, peering through holes in the dressing-room wall. The big arena is all an expanse of eager faces. The band strikes up a stirring ditty. A wave of excitement sweeps through the dingy quarters of the Garden. The show is on, and how delirious it all is!

Downstairs, the space behind the arena is a fascinating jostle of odd sights. The elephants come swaying up the runway from the basement and stand in line waiting their turn. Here is a cage of trained bears. In the background stands the dogcatcher's cart, attached to the famous kicking mule. From the ladies' dressing quarters come the aerial human butterflies in their wings and gauzy draperies. On the wall is a list of names, Mail Uncalled For. One of the names is "Toby Hamilton." That must mean old Toby, and we fear the letter will never be called for now, for Toby Hamilton, the famous old Barnum and Bailey press agent, who cleaned up more "free space" than any man who ever lived, died in 1916. Suddenly appears a person clad in flesh tights and a barrel, carrying a label announcing himself as The Common People. Someone thrusts a large sign into the hands of one of the amateur clowns, and he is thrust upon the arena, to precede the barrelled Common People round the sawdust circuit. He has hardly time to see what the sign says—something about "On Strike Against $100 Suits." The amateur clown is somewhat aghast at the huge display of friendly faces. Is he to try to be funny? Here is the flag-hung box, and he tries to see who is in it. He doesn't see either Wood, Pershing, or Mrs. Astor, who are not there; but a lot of wounded soldiers, who smile at him encouragingly. He feels better and proceeds, finding himself, with a start, just beneath some flying acrobats who are soaring in air, hanging by their teeth. Common People shouts to him to keep the sign facing toward the audience. The tour is made without palpable dishonour.

Things are now moving so fast it is hard to keep up with them. Pat Valdo is dressed as a prudish old lady with an enormous bustle. Escorted by the clown policeman and the two amateurs, Pat sets out, fanning himself demurely. Hullo! the bustle has detached itself from the old lady, but she proceeds, unconscious. The audience shouts with glee. Finally the cop sees what has happened and screams. The amateur clowns scream, too, and one of them, in a burst of inspiration, takes off his absurd hat to the bustle, which is now left yards behind. But Pat is undismayed, turns and beckons with his hand. The bustle immediately runs forward of its own accord and reattaches itself to the rear of the skirt. You see, there is a dwarf inside it. The two amateur clowns are getting excited by this time and execute some impromptu tumbling. One tackles the other and they roll over and over desperately. In the scuffle one loses both his hat and skull-cap and flees shamefast from the scene. It is asserted by our partner that "this went big." He swears it got a laugh. Pat Valdo hurries off to prepare for his boomerang throwing. Pat is a busy man, for he is not only a clown, but he and Mrs. Valdo also do wonderful stunts of their own on Ring Number One.

And there are moments of sheer poetry, too. Into the darkened arena, crossed by dazzling shafts of light, speeds a big white motor car. Bird Millman descends, tossing aside her cloak. "A fairy on a cobweb" the press agents call her, and as two humble clowns watch entranced through the peepholes in the big doors the phrase seems none too extravagant. See her, in a foam of short fluffy green skirts, twirl and tiptoe on the glittering wire, all grace and slenderness and agile enchantment. She bows in the dazzle of light and kisses her hands to the crowd. Then she hops into the big car and is borne back behind the scenes. Once behind the doors her gay vivacity ceases. She sits, wearily, several minutes, before getting out of the car. And then, later, comes Mlle. Leitzel. She, like all the other stars, is said to have "amazed all Europe." We don't know whether Europe is harder to amaze than America. Certainly no one could be more admiringly astounded than the amateur clowns gazing entranced through the crack of the doorway. To that nerve-tightening roll of drums she spins deliriously high up in giddy air, floating, a tiny human pin-wheel, in a shining cone of light. One can hear the crowd catch its breath. She walks back, all smiles, while her maid trots ahead saying something unintelligible. Her tall husband is waiting for her at the doorway. He catches her up like a child and carries her off, limp and exhausted. One of the clowns (irreverent creature) makes a piteous squawk and begs us to carry him to his dressing room.

A trained pig, trotting cheerfully round in search of tidbits, is retrieved from under the hooves of Mrs. Curtis's horse, which is about to go out and dance. The dogcatcher's wagon is drawn up ready to rush forth, and the trained terrier which accompanies it is leaping with excitement. He regards it as a huge lark, and knows his cue perfectly. When the right time comes he makes a dash for a clown dressed as an elderly lady and tears off her skirt. One of the amateurs was allowed to ride behind the kicking mule, but to his great chagrin the mule did not kick as well as usual. Here are Charley Chaplin and some others throwing enormous dice from a barrel. No matter how the dice are thrown they always turn up seven. Into this animated gamble the amateur clown enters with enjoyment. All round him the wildest capers are proceeding. The double-ended flivver is prancing about. John Barleycorn's funeral procession is going its way. "Give me plenty of space," says Charley Chaplin to us, "so the people can watch me." We do so, reverently, for Charley's antics are worth watching. We make a wild dash, and plan to do a tumble in imitation of Charley's. To our disappointment we find that instead of sliding our feet dig into the soft sawdust, and the projected collapse does not arrive. Intoxicated by the rich spice of circus odours, the booming calliope, the galloping horses, we hardly know what we are doing half the time. We hear Miss May Wirth, the Wonder Rider of the World, complaining bitterly that someone got in front of her when she was doing her particularly special stunt. We wonder dubiously whether we were the guilty one. Alas, it is all over but the washing up. Pat Valdo, gentlest of hosts, is taking off his trick hat with the water cistern concealed in it. He has a clean towel ready for his grateful pupils.

The band is playing "The Star-Spangled Banner," and all the clowns, in various stages of undress, stand at attention. Our little peep into the gay, good-hearted, courageous, and extraordinary world of the circus is over. Pat and his fellows will go on, twice a day, for the next six months. It takes patience and endurance. But it must be some consolation to know that nothing else in the world gives half as much pleasure to so many people.

HOUSE-HUNTING

A curious vertigo afflicts the mind of the house-hunter. In the first place, it is sufficiently maddening to see the settled homes of other happier souls, all apparently so firmly rooted in a warm soil of contentment while he floats, an unhappy sea-urchin, in an ocean of indecision. Furthermore, how confusing (to one who likes to feel himself somewhat securely established in a familiar spot) the startling panorama of possible places in which he visualizes himself. One day it is Great Neck, the next it is Nutley; one day Hollis, the next Englewood; one day Bronxville, and then Garden City. As the telephone rings, or the suasive accents of friendly realtors expound the joys and glories of various regions, his uneasy imagination flits hoppingly about the compass, conceiving his now vanished household goods reassembled and implanted in these contrasting scenes.

Startling scenarios are filmed in his reeling mind while he listens, over the tinkling wire, to the enumeration of rooms, baths, pantries, mortgages, commuting schedules, commodious closets, open fireplaces, and what not. In the flash and coruscation of thought he has transported his helpless family to Yonkers, or to Manhasset, or to Forest Hills, or wherever it may be, and tries to focus and clarify his vision of what it would all be like. He sees himself (in a momentary close-up) commuting on the bland and persevering Erie, or hastening hotly for a Liberty Street ferry, or changing at Jamaica (that mystic ritual of the Long Island brotherhood). For an instant he is settled again, with a modest hearth to return to at dusk ... and then the sorrowful compliment is paid him and he wonders how the impression got abroad that he is a millionaire.

There is one consoling aspect of his perplexity, however, and that is the friendly intercourse he has with high-spirited envoys who represent real estate firms and take him voyaging to see "properties" in the country. For these amiable souls he expresses his candid admiration. Just as when one contemplates the existence of the doctors one knows, one can never imagine them ill, so one cannot conceive of the friendly realtor as in any wise distressed or grieved by the problems of the home. There is something Olympian about them, happy creatures! They deal only in severely "restricted" tracts. They have a stalwart and serene optimism. Odd as it seems, one of these friends told us that some people are so malign as to waste the time of real estate men by going out to look at houses in the country without the slightest intention of "acting." As a kind of amusement, indeed! A harmless way of passing an afternoon, of getting perhaps a free motor ride and enjoying the novelty of seeing what other people's houses look like inside. But our friend was convinced of one humble inquirer's passionate sincerity when he saw him gayly tread the ice floes of rustic Long Island in these days of slush and slither.

How do these friends of ours, who see humanity in its most painful and distressing gesture (i.e., when it is making up its mind to part with some money), manage to retain their fine serenity and blitheness of spirit? They have to contemplate all the pathetic struggles of mortality, for what is more pathetic than the spectacle of a man trying to convince a real estate agent that he is not really a wealthy creature masking millions behind an eccentric pose of humility? Our genial adviser Grenville Kleiser, who has been showering his works upon us, has classified all possible mental defects as follows:

> *Too easy acquiescence*
> *A mental attitude of contradiction*
> *Undue skepticism*
> *A dogmatic spirit*
> *Lack of firmness of mind*
> *A tendency to take extreme views*

Love of novelty; that is, of what is foreign, ancient, unusual, or mysterious.

All these serious weaknesses of judgment may be discerned, in rapid rotation, in the mind of the house-hunter. It would be only natural, we think, if the real estate man were to tell him to go away and study Mr. Kleiser's "How to Build Mental Power." In the meantime, the vision of the home he had dreamed of becomes fainter and fainter in the seeker's mind—like the air of a popular song he has heard whistled about the streets, but does not know well enough to reproduce. How he envies the light-hearted robins, whose house-hunting consists merely in a gay flitting from twig to twig. Yet, even in his disturbance and nostalgia of spirit, he comforts himself with the common consolation of his cronies—"Oh, well, one always finds something"—and thus (in the words of good Sir Thomas Browne) teaches his haggard and unreclaimed reason to stoop unto the lure of Faith.

LONG ISLAND REVISITED

The anfractuosities of legal procedure having caused us to wonder whether there really were any such place as the home we have just bought, we thought we would go out to Salamis, L. I., and have a look at it. Of course we knew it had been there a few weeks ago, but the title companies do confuse one so. We had been sitting for several days in the office of the most delightful lawyer in the world (and if we did not fear that all the other harassed and beset creatures in these parts would instantly rush to lay their troubles in his shrewd and friendly bosom we would mention his name right here and do a little metrical pirouette in his honour)—we had been sitting there, we say, watching the proceedings, without the slightest comprehension of what was happening. It is really quite surprising, let us add, to find how many people are suddenly interested in some quiet, innocent-looking shebang nestling off in a quiet dingle in the country, and how, when it is to be sold, they all bob up from their coverts in Flushing, Brooklyn, or Long Island City, and have to be "satisfied." What floods of papers go crackling across the table, drawn out from those mysterious brown cardboard wallets; what quaint little jests pass between the emissaries of the title company and the legal counsel of the seller, jests that seem to bear upon the infirmity of human affairs and cause the well-wishing adventurer to wonder whether he had ever sufficiently pondered the strange tissue of mortal uncertainties that hides behind every earthly venture ... there was, for instance, occasional reference to a vanished gentleman who had once crossed the apparently innocent proscenium of our estate and had skipped, leaving someone six thousand dollars to the bad; this ingenious buccaneer was, apparently, the only one who did not have to be "satisfied." At any rate, we thought that we, who entered so modestly and obscurely into this whole affair, being only the purchaser, would finally satisfy ourself, too, by seeing if the property was still there.

Long Island and spring—the conjunction gives us a particular thrill. There are more beautiful places than the Long Island flats, but it was there that we earned our first pay envelope, and it was there that we first set up housekeeping; and as long as we live the station platform of Jamaica will move us strangely—not merely from one train to another, but also inwardly. There is no soil that receives a more brimming benison of sunshine than Long Island in late April. As the train moves across the plain it seems to swim in a golden tide

112

of light. Billboards have been freshly painted and announce the glories of phonographs in screaming scarlets and purples, or the number of miles that divide you from a Brooklyn department store. Out at Hillside the stones that demarcate the territory of an old-fashioned house are new and snowily whitewashed. At Hollis the trees are a cloud of violent mustard-yellow (the colour of a safety-matchbox label). Magnolias (if that is what they are) are creamy pink. Moving vans are bustling along the road. Across the wide fields of Bellaire there is a view of the brown woods on the ridge, turning a faint olive as the leaves gain strength. Gus Wuest's roadhouse at Queens looks inviting as of old, and the red-brown of the copper beeches reminds one of the tall amber beakers. Here is the little park by the station in Queens, the flag on the staff, the forsythia bushes the colour of scrambled eggs.

Is it the influence of the Belmont Park race track? There seem to be, in the smoking cars, a number of men having the air of those accustomed to associate (in a not unprofitable way) with horses. Here is one, a handsome person, who holds our eye as a bright flower might. He wears a flowing overcoat of fleecy fawn colour and a derby of biscuit brown. He has a gray suit and joyful socks of heavy wool, yellow and black and green in patterned squares which are so vivid they seem cubes rather than squares. He has a close-cut dark moustache, his shaven cheeks are a magnificent sirloin tint, his chin splendidly blue by the ministration of the razor. His shirt is blue with a stripe of sunrise pink, and the collar to match. He talks briskly and humorously to two others, leaning over in the seat behind them. As he argues, we see his brown low shoe tapping on the floor. One can almost see his foot think. It pivots gently on the heel, the toe wagging in air, as he approaches the climax of each sentence. Every time he drives home a point in his talk down comes the whole foot, softly, but firmly. He relights his cigar in the professional manner, not by inhaling as he applies the match, but by holding the burned portion in the flame, away from his mouth, until it has caught. His gold watch has a hunting case; when he has examined it, it shuts again with a fine rich snap, which we can hear even above the noise of the car.

On this early morning train there are others voyaging for amusement. Here are two golfing zealots, puffing pipes and discussing with amazing persistence the minutiæ of their sport. Their remarks are addressed to a very fashionable-looking curate, whose manners are superb. Whether he is going to play golf we know not; at any rate, he smiles mildly and politely to all they say.

113

Perhaps he is going round the course with them, in the hope of springing some ecclesiastical strategy while they are softened and chastened by the glee of the game. The name of their Maker, it is only fair to suspect, has more than once been mentioned on the putting green; and if it should slip out, the curate will seize the cue and develop it. In the meantime, one of the enthusiasts (while his companion is silenced in the act of lighting his pipe) is explaining to the cloth how his friend plays golf. "I'll tell you how he plays," he says. "Imagine him sitting down in a low chair and swinging a club. Then take the chair away and he still keeps the same position. That's what he looks like when he drives." The curate smiles at this and prepares his face to smile with equal gentleness when the other retorts.

After Floral Park the prospect becomes more plainly rural. The Mineola trolley zooms along, between wide fields of tilled brown earth. There is an occasional cow; here and there a really old barn and farmhouse standing, incongruously, among the settlements of modern kindling-wood cottages; and a mysterious agricultural engine at work with a spinning fly-wheel. Against the bright horizon stand the profiles of Garden City: the thin cathedral spire, the bulk of St. Paul's school, the white cupola of the hotel. The tree-lined vistas of Mineola are placidly simmering in the morning sun. A white dog with erect and curly tail trots very purposefully round the corner of the First National Bank. We think that we see the spreading leaves of some rhubarb plants in a garden; and there are some of those (to us very enigmatic, as we are no gardener) little glass window frames set in the soil, as though a whole house, shamed by the rent the owner wanted to charge, had sunk out of sight, leaving only a skylight.

As we leave East Williston we approach more interesting country, with a semblance of hills, and wooded thickets still brownly tapestried with the dry funeral of last year's leaves. On the trees the new foliage sways in little clusters, catching the light like the wings of perching green butterflies. Some of the buds are a coppery green, some a burning red, but the prevailing colour is the characteristic sulphur yellow of early spring. And now we are set down at Salamis, where the first and most surprising impression is of the unexpected abundance of competitive taxicabs. Having reached the terminus of our space, we can only add that we found our estate still there—and there are a few stalks of rhubarb surviving from an earlier plantation.

ON BEING IN A HURRY

New York is a perplexing city to loaf in. (Walt Whitman if he came back to Mannahatta would soon get brain fever.) During the middle hours of the day, at any rate, it is almost impossible to idle with the proper spirit and completeness. There is a prevailing bustle and skirmish that "exerts a compulsion," as President Wilson would say. The air is electric and nervous. We have often tried to dawdle gently about the neighbourhood of the City Hall in the lunch hour, to let the general form and spirit of that clearing among the cliffs sink into our mind, so that we could get some picture of it. We have sat under a big brown umbrella, to have our shoes shined, when we had nothing more important to do than go to the doughnut foundry on Park Row and try some of those delectable combinations of foods they have there, such as sponge cake with whipped cream and chocolate fudge. And in a few seconds we have found ourself getting all stirred up and crying loudly to the artist that we only wanted a once-over, as we had an important appointment. You have to put a very heavy brake on your spirit in downtown New York or you find yourself dashing about in a prickle of excitement, gloriously happy just to be in a hurry, without particularly caring whither you are hastening, or why.

One of the odd things about being in a hurry is that it seems so fiercely important when you yourself are the hurrier and so comically ludicrous when it is someone else. We see our friend Artaxerxes scorching up Church Street and we scream with laughter at him, because we know perfectly well that there is absolutely not one of his affairs important enough to cause him to buzz along like that. We look after him with a sort of mild and affectionate pity for a deluded creature who thinks that his concerns are of such glorious magnitude. And then, a few hours later, we find ourself on a subway car with only ten minutes to catch the train for Salamis at Atlantic Avenue. And what is our state of mind? We stand, gritting our teeth (we are too excited to sit, even if there were a seat) and holding our watch. The whole train, it seems to us, is occupied by invalids, tottering souls and lumbago cripples, who creep off at the stations as though five seconds made not the slightest difference. We glare and fume and could gladly see them all maced in sunder with battle-axes. Nothing, it seems to us, could soothe our bitter hunger for haste but to have a brilliant Lexington Avenue express draw up at the platform with not a soul in it. Out would step a polite guard, looking at his watch. "You want to catch a train at 5:27?" he asks. "Yes, sir, yes, sir; step aboard." All the other competitors are beaten back with knotted thongs and we are ushered to a seat. The bells go chiming in quick sequence up the length of the train and we are off at top speed, flying wildly past massed platforms of indignant people. We draw up at Atlantic Avenue, and the solitary passenger, somewhat appeased, steps off. "Compliments of the Interborough, sir," says the guard.

The commuter, urgently posting toward the 5:27, misses the finest flavour of the city's life, for it is in the two or three hours after office work is over that the town is at her best. What a spry and smiling mood is shown along the pavements, particularly on these clear, warm evenings when the dropping sun pours a glowing tide of soft rosy light along the cross-town streets. There is a cool lightness in the air; restaurants are not yet crowded (it is, let us say, a little after six) and beside snowy tablecloths the waiters stand indulgently with folded arms. Everybody seems in a blithe and spirited humour. Work is over for the day, and now what shall we do for amusement? This is the very peak of living, it seems to us, as we sally cheerily along the street. It is like the beginning of an O. Henry story. The streets are fluttering with beautiful women; light summer frocks are twinkling in the busy frolic air. Oh, to be turned loose at the corner of Broadway and Thirty-second Street at 6:15 o'clock of a June evening, with nothing to do but follow the smile of adventure to the utmost! Thirty-second, we might add, is our favourite street in New York. It saddens us to think that the old boarding house on the corner of Madison Avenue is vanished now and all those quaint and humorous persons dispersed. We can still remember the creak of the long stairs and the clink of a broken slab in the tiled flooring of the hall as one walked down to the dining room.

Affection for any particular street largely depends on the associations it has accumulated in one's mind. For several years most of our adventures in New York centred round Thirty-second Street; but its physique has changed so much lately that it has lost some of its appeal. We remember an old stone-yard that used to stand where the Pennsylvania Hotel is now, a queer jumbled collection of odd carvings and relics. At the front door there was a bust of Pan on a tall pedestal, which used to face us with a queer crooked grin twice a day, morning and evening. We had a great affection for that effigy, and even wrote a little piece about him in one of the papers, for which we got about $4 at a time when it was considerably needed. We used to say to ourself that some day when

116

we had a home in the country we would buy Pan and set him in a Long Island garden where he would feel more at home than in the dusty winds of Thirty-second Street. Time went on and we disappeared from our old haunts, and when we came back Pan had vanished, too. You may imagine our pleasure when we found him again the other day standing in front of a chop house on Forty-fourth Street.

But one great addition to the delights of the Thirty-second Street region is the new and shining white tunnel that leads one from the Penn Station subway platform right into the heart of what used (we think) to be called Greeley Square. It is so dazzling and candid in its new tiling that it seems rather like a vast hospital corridor. One emerges through the Hudson Tube station and perhaps sets one's course for a little restaurant on Thirty-fifth Street which always holds first place in our affection. It is somewhat declined from its former estate, for the upper floors, where the violent orchestra was and the smiling little dandruffian used to sing solos when the evening grew glorious, are now rented to a feather and ostrich plume factory. But the old basement is still there, much the same in essentials, by which we mean the pickled beet appetizers, the minestrone soup, the delicious soft bread with its brittle crust, and the thick slices of rather pale roast beef swimming in thin, pinkish gravy. And the three old French waiters, hardened in long experience of the frailties of mortality, smile to see a former friend. One, grinning upon us rather bashfully, recalls the time when there was a hilarious Oriental wedding celebrating in a private room upstairs and two young men insisted on going in to dance with the bride. He has forgiven various pranks, we can see, though he was wont to be outraged at the time. "Getting very stout," he says, beaming down at us. "You weigh a hundred pounds more than you used to." This is not merely cruel; it is untrue. We refrain from retorting on the growth of his bald spot.

CONFESSIONS OF A HUMAN GLOBULE

As a matter of fact, we find the evening subway jam very restful. Being neatly rounded in contour, with just a gentle bulge around the equatorial transit, we have devised a very satisfactory system. We make for the most crowded car we can find, and having buffeted our way in, we are perfectly serene. Once properly wedged, and provided no one in the immediate neighbourhood is doing anything with any garlic (it is well to avoid the vestibules if one is squeamish in that particular) we lift our feet off the floor, tuck them into the tail of our overcoat, and remain blissfully suspended in midair from Chambers Street to Ninety-sixth. The pressure of our fellow-passengers, powerfully impinging upon the globular perimeter we spoke of, keeps us safely elevated above the floor. We have had some leather stirrups sewed into the bottom of our overcoat, in which we slip our feet to keep them from dangling uncomfortably. Another feature of our technique is that we always go into the car with our arms raised and crossed neatly on our chest, so that they will not be caught and pinioned to our flanks. In that position, once we are gently nested among the elastic mass of genial humanity, it is easy to draw out from our waistcoat pocket our copy of Boethius's "Consolations of Philosophy" and really get in a little mental improvement. Or, if we have forgotten the book, we gently droop our head into our overcoat collar, lay it softly against the shoulder of the tall man who is always handy, and pass into a tranquil nescience.

The subway is a great consolation to the philosopher if he knows how to make the most of it. Think how many people one encounters and never sees again.

NOTES ON A FIFTH AVENUE BUS

Far down the valley of the Avenue the traffic lights wink in unison, green, yellow, red, changing their colours with well-drilled promptness. It is cold: a great wind flaps and tangles the flags; the tops of the buses are almost empty. That brisk April air seems somehow in key with the mood of the Avenue—hard, plangent, glittering, intensely material. It is a proud, exultant, exhilarating street; it fills the mind with strange liveliness. A magnificent pomp of humanity—what a flux of lacquered motors, what a twinkling of spats along the pavements! On what other of the world's great highways would one find churches named for the material of which they are built?—the Brick Church, the Marble Church! It is not a street for loitering—there is an eager, ambitious humour in its blood; one walks fast, revolving schemes of worldly dominion. Only on the terrace in front of the Public Library is there any temptation for tarrying and consideration. There one may pause and study the inscription—But Above All Things Truth Beareth Away the Victory ... of course the true eloquence of the words lies in the But. Much reason for that But, implying a previous contradiction—on the Avenue's part? Sometimes, pacing vigorously in that river of lovely pride and fascination, one might have suspected that other things bore away the victory—spats, diamond necklaces, smoky blue furs nestling under lovely chins.... Hullo! here is a sign, "Headquarters of the Save New York Committee." Hum! Save from what? There was a time when the great charm of New York lay in the fact that it didn't want to be saved. Who is it that the lions in front of the Public Library remind us of? We have so often pondered. Let's see: the long slanting brow, the head thrown back, the haughty and yet genial abstraction—to be sure, it's Vachel Lindsay!

We defy the most resolute philosopher to pass along the giddy, enticing, brilliant vanity of that superb promenade and not be just a little moved by worldly temptation.

119

SUNDAY MORNING

It was a soft, calm morning of sunshine and placid air. Clear and cool, it was "a Herbert Spencer of a day," as H. G. Wells once remarked. The vista of West Ninety-eighth Street, that engaging alcove in the city's enormous life, was all freshness and kempt tranquillity, from the gray roof of the old training ship at the river side up to the tall red spire near Columbus Avenue. This pinnacle, which ripens to a fine claret colour when suffused with sunset, we had presumed to be a church tower, but were surprised, on exploration, to find it a standpipe of some sort connected with the Croton water system.

Sunday morning in this neighbourhood has its own distinct character. There is a certain air of luxurious ease in the picture. One has a feeling that in those tall apartment houses there are a great many ladies taking breakfast in negligée. They are wearing (if one may trust the shop windows along Broadway) boudoir caps and mules. Mules, like their namesakes in the animal world, are hybrid things, the offspring of a dancing pump and a bedroom slipper. They are distinctly futile, but no matter, no matter. Wearing mules, however, is not a mere vanity; it is a form of physical culture, for these skimpish little things are always disappearing under the bed, and crawling after them keeps one slender. Again we say, no matter. This is no concern of ours.

Near Broadway a prosperous and opulently tailored costume emerges from an apartment house: cutaway coat, striped trousers, very long pointed patent leather shoes with lilac cloth tops. Within this gear, we presently see, is a human being, in the highest spirits. "All set!" he says, joining a group of similars waiting by a shining limousine. Among these, one lady of magnificently millinered aspect, and a smallish man in very new and shiny riding boots, of which he is grandly conscious. There are introductions. "Mr. Goldstone, meet Mrs. Silverware." They are met. There is a flashing of eyes. Three or four silk hats simultaneously leap into the shining air, are flourished and replaced. The observer is aware of the prodigious gayety and excitement of life. All climb into the car and roll away down Broadway. All save the little man in riding boots. He is left on the sidewalk, gallantly waving his hand. Come, we think, he is going riding. A satiny charger waits somewhere round the corner. We will follow and see. He slaps his hunting crop against his

120

glorious boots, which are the hue of quebracho wood. No; to our chagrin, he descends into the subway.

We sit on the shoeshining stand on Ninety-sixth Street, looking over the Sunday papers. Very odd, in the adjoining chairs men are busily engaged polishing shoes that have nobody in them, not visibly, at any rate. Perhaps Sir Oliver is right after all. While we are not watching, the beaming Italian has inserted a new pair of laces for us. Long afterward, at bedtime, we find that he has threaded them in that unique way known only to shoe merchants and polishers, by which every time they are tied and untied one end of the lace gets longer and the other shorter. Life is full of needless complexities. We descend the hill. Already (it is 9:45 a. m.) men are playing tennis on the courts at the corner of West End Avenue. A great wagon crammed with scarlet sides of beef comes stumbling up the hill, drawn, with difficulty, by five horses.

When we get down to the Ninety-Sixth Street pier we see the barque Windrush lying near by with the airy triangles of her rigging pencilled against the sky, and look amorously on the gentle curve of her strakes (if that is what they are). We feel that it would be a fine thing to be off soundings, greeting the bounding billow, not to say the bar-room steward; and yet, being a cautious soul of reservations all compact, we must admit that about the time we got abreast of New Dorp we would be homesick for our favourite subway station.

The pier, despite its deposit of filth, bales of old shoes, reeking barrels, scows of rubbish, sodden papers, boxes of broken bottles and a thick paste of dust and ash-powder everywhere, is a happy lounging ground for a few idlers on Sunday morning. A large cargo steamer, the Eclipse, lay at the wharf, standing very high out of the water. Three small boys were watching a peevish old man tending his fishing lines, fastened to wires with little bells on them. "What do you catch here?" we said. Just then one of the little bells gave a cracked tinkle and the angler pulled up a small fish, wriggling briskly, about three inches long. This seemed to anger him. He seemed to consider himself in some way humiliated by the incident. He grunted. One of the small boys was tactful. "Oh, gee!" he said. "Sometimes you catch fish that long," indicating a length which began at about a yard and diminished to about eighteen inches as he meditated. "I don't know what kind they are," he said. "They're not trouts, but some other kind of fish."

This started the topic of relative sizes, always fascinating to small boys. "That's a pretty big boat," said one, craning up at the tall stem

121

of the Eclipse. "Oh, gee, that ain't big!" said another. "You ought to see some of the Cunard boats, the Olympic or the Baltic."

On Riverside Drive horseback riders were cantering down the bridlepath, returning from early outings. The squirrels, already grossly overfed, were brooding languidly that another day of excessive peanuts was at hand. Behind a rapidly spinning limousine pedalled a grotesquely humped bicyclist, using the car as a pacemaker. He throbbed fiercely just behind the spare tire, with his face bent down into a rich travelling cloud of gasoline exhaust. An odd way of enjoying one's self! Children were coming out in troops, with their nurses, for the morning air. Here was a little boy with a sailor hat, and on the band a gilt legend that was new to us. Instead of the usual naval slogan, it simply said Democracy. This interested us, as later in the day we saw another, near the goldfish pond in Central Park. Behind the cashier's grill of a Broadway drug store the good-tempered young lady was reading Zane Grey. "I love his books," she said, "but they make me want to break loose and go out West."

VENISON PASTY

The good old days are gone, we have been frequently and authoritatively assured; and yet, sitting in an agreeable public on William Street where the bright eye of our friend Harold Phillips discerned venison pasty on the menu, and listening to a seafaring man describe a recent "blow" off Hatteras during which he stood four hours up to his waist in the bilges, and watching our five jocund companions dismiss no less than twenty-one beakers of cider, we felt no envy whatever for the ancients of the Mermaid Tavern. After venison pasty, and feeling somewhat in the mood of Robin Hood and Friar Tuck, we set off with our friend Endymion for a stroll through the wilderness. The first adventure of note that we encountered was the curb market on Broad Street, where we stood entranced at the merry antics of the brokers. This, however, is a spectacle that no layman can long contemplate and still deem himself sane. That sea of flickering fingers, the hubbub of hoarse cries, and the enigmatic gestures of youths framed in the open windows gave an impression of something fierce and perilous happening. Endymion, still deeming himself in Sherwood Forest, insisted that this was the abode of the Sheriff of Nottingham. "Stout deeds are toward!" he cried. "These villain wights have a damsel imprisoned in yonder keep!" With difficulty we restrained him from pressing to the rescue of the lady (for indeed we could see her, comely enough, appearing now and then at one of the windows; and anon disappearing, abashed at the wild throng). But gradually we realized that no such dire matter was being transacted, for the knights, despite occasional spasms of hot gesticulating fury, were mild and meant her no ill. One, after a sudden flux of business concerning (it seemed) 85 shares of Arizona Copper, fell suddenly placid, and was eating chocolate ice cream from a small paper plate. Young gallants, wearing hats trimmed with variegated brightly coloured stuffs (the favours of their ladies, we doubted not), were conferring together, but without passion or rancour.

We have a compact with our friend Endymion that as soon as either of us spends money for anything not strictly necessary he must straightway return to the office. After leaving the curb market, we found ourselves in a basement bookshop on Broadway, and here Endymion fell afoul of a copy of Thomas Hardy's "Wessex Poems," illustrated by the author. Piteously he tried to persuade us that it was a matter of professional advancement to him to have this book;

moreover, he said, he had just won five dollars at faro (or some such hazard) so that he was not really spending money at all; but we countered all his sophisms with slogging rhetoric. He bought the book, and so had to return to the office in disgrace.

We fared further, having a mind to revisit the old Eastern Hotel, down by the South Ferry, of whose cool and dusky bar-room we had pleasant memories in times gone by; but we found to our distress that this also, like many more of our familiar landmarks, is a prey to the house-wrecker, and is on its way to become an office building. On our way back up Broadway it occurred to us to revisit what we have long considered one of the most impressive temples in our acquaintance, the lobby of the Telephone and Telegraph Building, on Dey Street. Here, passing by the enticing little terrace with brocaded chairs and soft lights where two gracious ladies sit to interview aspiring telephone débutantes, one stands in a dim golden glow, among great fluted pillars and bowls of softly burning radiance swung (like censers) by long chains. Occasionally there is an airy flutter, a bell clangs, bronze doors slide apart, and an elevator appears, in charge of a chastely uniformed priestess. Lights flash up over this dark little cave which stands invitingly open: UP, they say, LOCAL 1-13. The door-sill of the cave shines with a row of golden beads (small lights, to guide the foot)—it is irresistible. There is an upward impulse about the whole place: the light blossoms upward from the hanging translucent shells: people step gently in, the doors close, they are not seen again. It is the temple of the great American religion, Going Up. The shining gold stars in the ceiling draw the eye aloft. The temptation is too great. We step into the little bronze crypt, say "Thirteen" at a venture, and are borne softly and fluently up. Then, of course, we have to come down again, past the wagons of spring onions on Fulton Street, and back to the office.

GRAND AVENUE, BROOKLYN

We have always been a strong partisan of Brooklyn, and when we found ourself, in company with Titania, set down in the middle of a golden afternoon with the vista of Grand Avenue before us, we felt highly elated. Just how these two wayfarers chanced to be deposited in that quiet serenity, so far from their customary concerns, is not part of the narrative.

There are regions of Brooklyn, we have always felt, that are too good to be real. Placid stretches of streets, with baby carriages simmering in the sun, solid and comfortable brownstone houses exhaling a prosperous condition of life, tranquil old-fashioned apothecaries' shops without soda fountains, where one peers in and sees only a solitary customer turning over the pages of a telephone book. It is all rather like a chapter from a story, and reminds us of a passage in "The Dynamiter" where some untroubled faubourgs of London are winningly described.

Titania was wearing a little black hat with green feathers. She looked her best, and was not unaware of it. Our general plan, when destiny suddenly plumps us into the heart of Brooklyn, is to make our way toward Fulton Street, which is a kind of life-line. Once on Fulton Street we know our way. Moreover, Fulton Street has admirable second-hand bookshops. Nor do we ever forget that it was at the corner of Fulton and Cranberry streets that "Leaves of Grass" was set up, in the spring of 1855, Walt doing a good deal of the work himself. The only difficulty about getting to Fulton Street is that people will give you such contradictory instruction. One will tell you to go this way; the next will point in the opposite direction. It is as though Brooklynites suspect the presence of a stranger, and do not wish their sacred secrets to be discovered. There is a deep, mysterious freemasonry among the residents of this genial borough.

At the corner of Grand and Greene avenues we thought it well to ask our way. A lady was standing on the corner, lost in pleasant drowse. April sunshine shimmered all about: trees were bustling into leaf, a wagonload of bananas stood by the curb and the huckster sang a gay, persuasive madrigal. We approached the lady, and Titania spoke gently: "Can you tell me——" The lady screamed, and leaped round in horror, her face stricken with fearful panic. She gasped and tottered. We felt guilty and cruel. "We were not meditating an attack," we said, "but just wanted to ask you the way to Fulton Street." Perhaps the poor soul's nerves were unstrung, for she gave us instruction that we felt instinctively to be wrong. Had we gone as she said (we now see by studying the map) we would have debouched into Wallabout Bay. But undoubtedly it was the protective instinct of the Brooklynite, on guard before strangers. Is there some terrific secret in Brooklyn that all residents know about but which must never be revealed to outsiders?

Making a mental note not to speak too suddenly at the next encounter, the two cheerful derelicts drifted along the sunny coast of Grand Avenue. A shining and passionless peace presided over the streets. A gentle clop-clop of hooves came trotting down the way: here was a man driving a white horse in a neat rubber-tired buggy without a top. He leaned back and smiled to himself as he drove along. Life did not seem to be the same desperate venture it appears round about Broadway and Wall Street. Who can describe the settled amiability of those rows of considerable brown houses, with their heavy oak doors, their pots of daisies on the stoop, their clear window panes, and now and then the face of a benignant grandmother peeping from behind lace curtains. The secret of Brooklyn, perhaps, is contentment, and its cautious residents do not want the rest of us to know too much about it, lest we all flock over there in swarms.

We then came to the bustle of Fulton Street, which deserves a book in itself. Some day we want to revisit a certain section of Fulton Street where (if we remember rightly) a rotisserie and a certain bookstore conspire to make one of the pleasantest haunts in our experience. We don't know exactly what the secret of Brooklyn may be, but we are going to spend some time over there this spring and lie in wait for it.

ON WAITING FOR THE CURTAIN TO GO UP

We often wonder whether people are really as human as they appear, or is it only our imagination? Everybody, we suggest, thinks of others as being excessively human, with all the frailties and crotchets appertaining to that curious condition. But each of us also (we are not dogmatic on this matter) seems to regard himself as existing on a detached plane of observation, exempt (save in moments of vivid crisis) from the strange whims of humanity en masse.

For example, consider the demeanour of people at a theatre while waiting for the curtain to go up. To note the censoriousness with which they study each other, one concludes that each deems himself (herself) singularly blessed as the repository of human correctness.

Incidentally, why is it that one gets so thirsty at the theatre? We never get thirsty at the movies, or not nearly so thirsty. The other evening we drank seven paper cups full of water in the intermissions of a four-act play.

The presence of people sitting behind one is the reason (we fancy) for a great deal of the queer antics that take place while one is waiting for the curtain to rise, particularly when it is twenty minutes late in going up as it was at a certain theatre the other evening. People behind one have a horrible advantage. One knows that they can hear everything you say, unless you whisper it in a furtive manner, which makes them suspect things far worse than any one would be likely to say in a Philadelphia theatre, except, of course, on the stage. The fact that you know they can overhear you, and intend to do so, leads one on to make the most outrageous, cynical, and scoffish remarks, particularly to denounce with fury a play that you may be enjoying quite passably well. All over the house you will hear (after the first act) men saying to their accompanying damsels, "How outrageously clumsy that act was. I can't conceive how the director let it get by." Now they only say this because they think it will make the people behind feel ashamed for having enjoyed such a botch. But does it? The people in the row behind immediately begin to praise the play vigorously, for the benefit of the people behind them; and in a minute you see the amusing spectacle of the theatre cheering and damning by alternate rows.

Here and there you will see a lady whispering something to her escort, and will notice how ladies always look backward over a lily shoulder while whispering. They want to see what effect this whispering will have on the people behind. There is a deep-rooted feud between every two rows in an audience. The front row, having nobody to hate (except possibly the actors), take it out in speculating why on earth anybody can want to sit in the boxes, where they can see nothing.

What the boxes think about we are not sure. We never sat in a box except at a burlicue.

And then a complete essay might be written on the ads in the theatre program—what high-spirited ads they are! How full of the savour and luxurious tang of the beau monde! How they insist on saying specialité instead of specialty!

Well, all we meant to say when we began was, the heroine was Only Fair—by which we mean to say she was beautiful and nothing else.

MUSINGS OF JOHN MISTLETOE

It was old John Mistletoe, we think, in his "Book of Deplorable Facts," discussing the congenial topic of "Going to Bed" (or was it in his essay on "The Concinnity of Washerwomen?") said something like this:

> Life passes by with deplorable rapidity. *Post commutatorem sedet horologium terrificum*, behind the commuter rideth the alarm clock, no sooner hath he attained to the office than it is time for lunch, no sooner hath lunch been dispatched than it is time to sign those dictated letters, no sooner this accomplished, 'tis time to hasten trainward. The essential thing, then, is not to let one's experiences flow irrevocably past like a river, but to clutch and hold them, thoughtfully, long enough to examine and, in a manner, sieve them, to halt them in the mind for meditation. The relentless fluidity of life, the ease with which it vanisheth down the channel of the days, is the problem the thoughtful man must deal with. The urgent necessity is to dam the stream here and there so we can go swimming in it.

> Time is a breedy creature: the minutes propagate hours, the hours beget days, the days raise huge families of months, and before we know it we are crowded out of this sweet life by mere surplus of Time's offspring. This is a brutish Malthusianism which must be adamantly countered. Therefore it is my counsel that every man, ere he retire for the night and commit his intellect to inscrutable nothingness, do let it hop abroad for a little freedom. Life must be taken with a grain of saltation: let the spirit dance a measure or two ere it collapse. For this purpose it is my pleasure, about the hour of midnight, to draw a jug of cider from the keg and a book from the shelf. I choose some volume ill written and stupidly conceived, to set me in conceit with myself. I read a few pages, and then apply myself to the composition of verses. These done, I burn them, and go to bed with a cheerful spirit.

THE WORLD'S MOST FAMOUS ORATION

Address to An Employer Upon Demanding a Raise, or, The Battle of Manila Envelopes

As Planned

I think you will admit, sir, that the quality of my work during the last two years has been such that my services could not easily be replaced. I speak more in pain than in anger when I say that it has been a matter of profound surprise to me to note that you have not seen fit to acknowledge my value to the firm in some substantial way. I think I may say that I have been patient. I have continued my efforts with unremitting zeal, and I think I may flatter myself that my endeavors have not been without result. I have here, carefully tabulated, a memorandum of the increased profits in my department during the last twelve months, due in great part to my careful management. I am sorry to have to force you into a decision, but I think I owe it to myself to say candidly that unless you see the matter in the same way that I do I shall feel obliged to deprive the firm of my services.

As Delivered

If you are not too busy, sir, there is one other matter—in fact, the truth of the matter in fact is exactly—well, sir, I was precisely wondering whether—of course I know this is a bad time—indeed I have been very pleased to see business picking up a bit lately, and I am sure my own department has been—but to tell you the truth, sir, I have been wondering—of course it is just as you think best and I wouldn't think of insisting, but after all, perhaps I have made a mistake in mentioning it, but I was thinking that possibly you might bear in mind the idea of a possible future raise in salary at some future time.

ON LAZINESS

To-day we rather intended to write an essay on Laziness, but were too indolent to do so.

The sort of thing we had in mind to write would have been exceedingly persuasive. We intended to discourse a little in favour of a greater appreciation of Indolence as a benign factor in human affairs.

It is our observation that every time we get into trouble it is due to not having been lazy enough. Unhappily, we were born with a certain fund of energy. We have been hustling about for a number of years now, and it doesn't seem to get us anything but tribulation. Henceforward we are going to make a determined effort to be more languid and demure. It is the bustling man who always gets put on committees, who is asked to solve the problems of other people and neglect his own.

The man who is really, thoroughly, and philosophically slothful is the only thoroughly happy man. It is the happy man who benefits the world. The conclusion is inescapable.

We remember a saying about the meek inheriting the earth. The truly meek man is the lazy man. He is too modest to believe that any ferment and hubbub of his can ameliorate the earth or assuage the perplexities of humanity.

O. Henry said once that one should be careful to distinguish laziness from dignified repose. Alas, that was a mere quibble. Laziness is always dignified, it is always reposeful. Philosophical laziness, we mean. The kind of laziness that is based upon a carefully reasoned analysis of experience. Acquired laziness. We have no respect for those who were born lazy; it is like being born a millionaire: they cannot appreciate their bliss. It is the man who has hammered his laziness out of the stubborn material of life for whom we chant praise and allelulia.

The laziest man we know—we do not like to mention his name, as the brutal world does not yet recognize sloth at its community value—is one of the greatest poets in this country; one of the keenest satirists; one of the most rectilinear thinkers. He began life in the customary hustling way. He was always too busy to enjoy himself.

131

He became surrounded by eager people who came to him to solve their problems. "It's a queer thing," he said sadly; "no one ever comes to me asking for help in solving my problems." Finally the light broke upon him. He stopped answering letters, buying lunches for casual friends and visitors from out of town, he stopped lending money to old college pals and frittering his time away on all the useless minor matters that pester the good-natured. He sat down in a secluded café with his cheek against a seidel of dark beer and began to caress the universe with his intellect.

The most damning argument against the Germans is that they were not lazy enough. In the middle of Europe, a thoroughly disillusioned, indolent and delightful old continent, the Germans were a dangerous mass of energy and bumptious push. If the Germans had been as lazy, as indifferent, and as righteously laissez-fairish as their neighbours, the world would have been spared a great deal.

People respect laziness. If you once get a reputation for complete, immovable, and reckless indolence the world will leave you to your own thoughts, which are generally rather interesting.

> Doctor Johnson, who was one of the world's great philosophers, was lazy. Only yesterday our friend the Caliph showed us an extraordinarily interesting thing. It was a little leather-bound notebook in which Boswell jotted down memoranda of his talks with the old doctor. These notes he afterward worked up into the immortal Biography. And lo and behold, what was the very first entry in this treasured little relic?

Doctor Johnson told me in going to Ilam from Ashbourne, 22 September, 1777, that the way the plan of his Dictionary came to be addressed to Lord Chesterfield was this: He had neglected to write it by the time appointed. Dodsley suggested a desire to have it addressed to Lord C. Mr. J. laid hold of this as an excuse for delay, that it might be better done perhaps, and let Dodsley have his desire. Mr. Johnson said to his friend, Doctor Bathurst: "Now if any good comes of my addressing to Lord Chesterfield it will be ascribed to deep policy and address, when, in fact, it was only a casual excuse for laziness."

Thus we see that it was sheer laziness that led to the greatest triumph of Doctor Johnson's life, the noble and memorable letter to Chesterfield in 1775.

Mind your business is a good counsel; but mind your idleness also. It's a tragic thing to make a business of your mind. Save your mind to amuse yourself with.

The lazy man does not stand in the way of progress. When he sees progress roaring down upon him he steps nimbly out of the way. The lazy man doesn't (in the vulgar phrase) pass the buck. He lets the buck pass him. We have always secretly envied our lazy friends. Now we are going to join them. We have burned our boats or our bridges or whatever it is that one burns on the eve of a momentous decision.

Writing on this congenial topic has roused us up to quite a pitch of enthusiasm and energy.

TEACHING THE PRINCE TO TAKE NOTES

The Prince of Wales probably suffers severely during his tours abroad, for he is a shy youth; but he also makes many friends, for he is a delightfully simple and agreeable person. When we used to see him he looked a good deal like the traditional prince of the fairy tales, for he was a slender boy with yellow hair, and blue eyes, and a quick pink blush. And we feel toward him the friendly sense of superiority that the college alumnus always feels toward the man who was a freshman when he himself was a senior; for the prince and ourself stood in that relation a few years ago at a certain haunt of letters.

There was a course of lectures on history that we were to attend. It was a popular course, and the attendance was large. Arriving late at the first lecture the room was packed, and we could see from the door that there was only one empty seat. This happened to be in the very front row, and wondering how it was that so desirable a place had not been seized we hastened to it. The lecturer was a swift talker, and we fell to taking notes busily. Not for some minutes did we have a chance to scrutinize our surroundings. We then saw that in the adjoining chair sat the prince, and surmised that no one had wanted to take the chair for fear of being twitted by his companions for a supposed desire to hobnob with royalty.

If we remember correctly, it was the prince's first term of college life. The task of taking notes from a rapid-fire lecturer was plainly one to which he was not accustomed, and as he wrestled with his notebook we could see that he had not learned the art of considering the lecturer's remarks and putting down only the gist of them, in some abbreviated system of his own, as every experienced student learns. Grant Robertson, the well-known historian, was lecturing on English constitutional documents, and his swift and informal utterance was perfectly easy to summarize if one knew how to get down the important points and neglect the rest. But the unhappy prince, desperately eager to do the right thing in this new experience, was trying to write down every word. If, for instance, Mr. Robertson said (in a humorous aside), "Henry VIII was a sinful old man with a hobby of becoming a widower," the experienced listener would jot down something like this: H 8, self-made widower. But we could see that the prince was laboriously copying out the sentence in full. And naturally, by the end of a few paragraphs, he was hopelessly behind. But he scribbled away industriously, doing his best. He realized, however, that he had not quite got the hang of the thing, and at the end of the lecture he turned to us with most agreeable bashfulness and asked if we would lend him our notebook, so that he could get down the points that he had missed. We did so, and briefly explained our own system of abbreviating. We noticed that in succeeding sessions our royal neighbour did very much better, learning in some measure to discriminate between what was advisable to note down and what was mere explanatory matter or persiflage on the part of the lecturer. But (if we must be candid) we would not recommend him as a newspaper reporter. And, indeed, the line of work to which he has been called does not require quite as intense concentration as that of a cub on what Philip Gibbs calls "The Street of Adventure."

No one could come in contact with the prince without liking him, for his bashful, gentle, and teachable nature is very winning. We remember with a certain amusement the time that Grant Robertson got off one of his annual gags to the effect that, according to the principle of strict legitimacy, there were in Europe several hundred (we forget the figure) people with a greater right to the British throne than the family at present occupying it. The roomful of students roared with genial mirth, and the unhappy prince blushed in a way that young girls used to in the good old days of three-piece bathing suits.

A CITY NOTEBOOK

(Philadelphia)

It would be hard to find a more lovely spot in the flush of a summer sunset than Wister Woods. Old residents of the neighbourhood say that the trees are not what they were fifteen and twenty years ago; the chestnuts have died off; even some of the tall tulip-poplars are a little bald at the top, and one was recently felled by a gale. But still that quiet plateau stands in a serene hush, flooded with rich orange glow on a warm evening. The hollyhocks in the back gardens of Rubicam Street are scarlet and Swiss-cheese-coloured and black; and looking across the railroad ravine one sees crypts and aisles of green as though in the heart of some cathedral of the great woods.

Belfield Avenue, which bends through the valley in a curve of warm thick yellow dust, will some day be boulevarded into a spick-and-span highway for motors. But now it lies little trafficked, and one might prefer to have it so, for in the stillness of the evening the birds are eloquent. The thrushes of Wister Woods, which have been immortalized by T. A. Daly in perhaps the loveliest poem ever written in Philadelphia, flute and whistle their tantalizing note, while the song sparrow echoes them with his confident, challenging call. Down behind the dusty sumac shrubbery lies the little blue-green cottage said to have been used by Benjamin West as a studio. In a meadow beside the road two cows were grazing in the blue shadow of overhanging woodland.

Over the road leans a flat outcrop of stone, known locally as "The Bum's Rock." An antique philosopher of those parts assured the wayfarer that it is named for a romantic vagabond who perished there by the explosion of a can of Bohemian goulash which he was heating over a small fire of sticks; but one doubts the tale. Our own conjecture is that it is named for Jacob Boehm, the oldtime brewer of Germantown, who predicted in his chronicles that the world would come to an end in July, 1919. From his point of view he was not so far wrong.

Above Boehm's Rock, in a grassy level among the trees, a merry little circle of young ladies was sitting round a picnic supper. The twilight grew darker and fireflies began to twinkle. In the steep curve of the Cinder and Bloodshot (between Fisher's and Wister stations) a cheerful train rumbled, with its engine running

136

backward just like a country local. Its bright shaft of light wavered among the tall tree trunks. One would not imagine that it was less than six miles to the City Hall.

A quarter to one a. m., and a hot, silent night. As one walks up Chestnut Street a distant roaring is heard, which rapidly grows louder. The sound has a note of terrifying menace. Then, careering down the almost deserted highway, comes a huge water-tank, throbbing like an airplane. A creamy sheet of water, shot out at high pressure, floods the street on each side, dashing up on the pavements. A knot of belated revellers in front of the Adelphia Hotel, standing in mid-street, to discuss ways and means of getting home, skip nimbly to one side, the ladies lifting up their dresses with shrill squeaks of alarm as the water splashes round them. Pedestrians plodding quietly up the street cower fearfully against the buildings, while a fine mist envelops them.

After the tank comes, more leisurely, a squad of brooms. The street is dripping, every sewer opening clucks and gurgles with the falling water. There is something unbelievably humorous in the way that roaring Niagara of water dashes madly down the silent street. There is a note of irony in it, too, for the depressed enthusiasts who have been sitting all evening in a restaurant over lemonade and ginger ale. Perhaps the chauffeur is a prohibitionist gone mad.

While eating half a dozen doughnuts in a Broad Street lunchroom at one o'clock in the morning, we mused happily about our friends all tucked away in bed, sound asleep. There is one in particular on whom we thought with serene pleasure. It was charming to think of that delightful, argumentative, contradictory, volatile person, his active mind stilled in the admirable reticence of slumber. He, so endlessly speculatory, so full of imaginative enthusiasms and riotous intuitions and troubled zeals concerning humanity, lost in a beneficent swoon of unconsciousness! We could not just say why, but we broke into chuckles to think of him lying there, not denying any of our statements, absolutely and positively saying nothing. To have one's friends asleep now and then is very refreshing.

Off Walnut Street, below Fifth, and just east of the window where that perfectly lovely damsel sits operating an adding machine—why is it, by the way, that the girls who run adding machines are always so marvellously fair? Is there some secret virtue in the process of adding that makes one lovely? We feel sure that a subtracting engine would not have that subtle beautifying effect—just below Fifth Street, we started to say, there runs a little alley called (we

137

believe) De Silver Court. It is a sombre little channel between high walls and barred windows, but it is a retreat we recommend highly to hay fever sufferers. For in one of the buildings adjoining there seems to be a warehouse of some company that makes an "aromatic disinfector." Wandering in there by chance, we stood delighted at the sweet medicinal savour that was wafted on the air. It had a most cheering effect upon our emunctory woes, and we lingered so long, in a meditative and healing ecstasy, that young women immured in the basement of the aromatic warehouse began to peer upward from the barred windows of their basement and squeak with astonished and nervous mirth. We blew a loud salute and moved away.

We entered a lunchroom on Broad Street for our favourite breakfast of coffee and a pair of crullers. It was strangely early and only a few of the flat-arm chairs were occupied. After dispatching the rations we carefully filled our pipe. With us we had a copy of an agreeable book, "The Calamities and Quarrels of Authors." It occurred to us that here, in the brisk serenity of the morning, would be a charming opportunity for a five-minute smoke and five pages of reading before attacking the ardours and endurances of the day. Lovingly we applied the match to the fuel. We began to read:

> Of all the sorrows in which the female character may participate, there are few more affecting than those of an authoress——

A stern, white-coated official came over to us and tapped us on the shoulder.

"There's a sign behind you," he said.

We looked, guiltily, and saw:

POSITIVELY
NO SMOKING

The cocoateria on Eighth Street closes at one a. m. Between twelve-thirty and closing time it is full of busy eaters, mostly the night shift from the Chestnut Street newspaper offices and printing and engraving firms in the neighbourhood. Ham and eggs blossom merrily. The white-coated waiters move in swift, stern circuit. Griddle cakes bake with amazing swiftness toward the stroke of one. Little dishes of baked beans stand hot and ready in the steam-chest. The waiter punches your check as he brings your frankfurters and coffee. He adds another perforation when you get your ice cream. Then he comes back and punches it again.

138

"Here," you cry, "let it alone and stop bullying it!"

"Sorry, brother," he says. "I forgot that peach cream was fifteen cents."

One o'clock. They lock the door and turn out the little gas jet where smokers light up. As the tables empty the chairs are stacked up on top. And if it is a clear warm evening the customers smoke a final weed along the Chestnut Street doorsteps, talking together in a cheery undertone.

No man has ever started upon a new cheque-book without a few sourly solemn thoughts.

In the humble waters of finance wherein we paddle we find that a book of fifty cheques lasts us about four months, allowing for two or three duds when we start to make out a foil payable to bearer (self) and decide to renounce that worthy ambition and make it out to the gas company instead.

It occurs to us that if Bunyan had been writing "Pilgrim's Progress" nowadays instead of making Christian encounter lions in the path he would have substituted gas meters, particularly the quarter-in-the-slot kind that one finds in a seaside cottage. However——

Four months is quite a long time. It may be weak of us, but we can never resist wondering as we survey that flock of empty cheques just what adventures our bank account is going to undergo during that period, and whether our customary technique of being aloof with the receiving teller and genial and commentary with the paying ditto is the right one. We always believe in keeping a paying teller in a cheerful frame of mind. We would never admit to him that we think it is going to rain. We say, rather, "Well, it may blow over," and try not to surmise how many hundreds there are in the pile at his elbow. Probably we think the explanation for the really bizarre architecture of our bank is to keep depositors' attention from the money. Unquestionably Walt Whitman's tomb over in Harleigh—Walt's vault—was copied from our bank.

The cheques in our book are blue. We have always regretted this. If we had known it beforehand perhaps we would have inflicted our problems upon another bank. Because there are so many more interesting colours for cheques, tints upon which the ink shows up in a more imposing manner. A pale pink or cream-coloured cheque for $2.74 looks much more exciting than a blue cheque for $25. We

139

have known gray, pink, white, brown, green, and salmon-coloured cheques. A friend of ours once showed us one that was a bright orange, but refused to let us handle it. But yellow is the colour that appeals to us most strongly. When we were very young and away from home our monthly allowance, the amount of which we shall not state, but it cost us less effort than any money we ever received since, came to us by way of pale primrose-coloured cheques. For, after all, there are no cheques like those one used to get from one's father. We hope the Urchin will think so some day.

We like to pay homage to the true artist in all lines. At the corner of Market and Marshall streets—between Sixth and Seventh—the collar-clasp orator has his rostrum, and it seems to us that his method of harangue has the quality of genuine art. He does not bawl or try to terrify or bully his audience into purchase as do the auctioneers of the "pawnbrokers' outlets." How gently, how winningly, how sweetly he pleads the merits of his little collar clasp! And there is shrewd imagination in his attention-catching device, which is a small boy dressed in black, wearing a white hood of cheesecloth that hides his face. This peculiar silent figure, with a touch of mystery about it, serves to keep the crowd wondering until the oration begins.

With a smile, with infinite ingratiation and gentle persuasion, our friend exhibits the merits of his device which does away with the traditional collar-button. His art is to make the collar-button seem a piteous, almost a tragic thing. His eyes swim with unshed tears as he describes the discomfort of the man whose collar, fastened by the customary button, cannot be given greater freedom on a hot, muggy day. He shows, by exhibition on his own person, the exquisite relief afforded by the adjustable collar clasp. "When the day grows cool," he says, "when you begin to enjoy yourself and want your collar tighter, you just loosen the clasp, slide the tabs closer together, and there you are. And no picking at your tie to get the knot undone. Now, how many of you men have spoiled an expensive tie by picking at it? Your fingers come in contact with the fibres of the silk and the first thing you know the tie is soiled. This little clasp"—and he casts a beam of affection upon it—"saves your tie, it saves your collar, and it saves your patience." A note of yearning pathos comes into his agreeable voice, and he holds out a handful of the old-fashioned collar-buttons. "You men are wearing the same buttons your great-grandfathers wore. Don't you want to get out of collar slavery? Don't you want to quit working your face all out of shape struggling with a collar-button? Now as this is a manufacturing demonstration——"

On a warm evening nothing is more pleasant than a ride on the front platform of the Market Street L, with the front door open. As the train leaves Sixty-ninth Street it dips down the Millbourne bend and the cool, damp smell of the Cobb's Creek meadows gushes through the car. Then the track straightens out for a long run toward the City Hall. Roaring over the tree tops, with the lights of movies and shops glowing up from below, a warm typhoon makes one lean against it to keep one's footing. The airy stations are lined by girls in light summer dresses, attended by their swains. The groan of the wheels underfoot causes a curious tickling in the soles of the feet as one stands on the steel platform.

This groan rises to a shrill scream as the train gathers speed between stations, gradually diminishing to a reluctant grumble as the cars come to a stop. In the distance, in a peacock-blue sky, the double gleam of the City Hall tower shines against the night. Down on the left is the hiss and clang of West Philadelphia station, with the long, dim, amber glow of the platform and belated commuters pacing about. Then the smoky dive across the Schuylkill and the bellow of the subway.

From time to time humanity is forced to revise its customary notions in the interests of truth. This is always painful.

It is an old fetich that the week-end in summer is a time for riotous enjoyment, of goodly cheer and mirthful solace. A careful examination of human beings during this hebdomadal period of carnival leads us to question the doctrine.

When we watch the horrors of discomfort and vexation endured by simple-hearted citizens in pursuit of a light-hearted Saturday and Sunday, we often wonder how it is that humanity will so gleefully inflict upon itself sufferings which, if they were imposed by some taskmaster, would be called atrocious.

We observe, for instance, women and children standing sweltering in the aisles of trains during a two-hour run to the seashore. We observe the number of drownings, motor accidents, murders, and suicides that take place during the Saturday to Monday period. We observe families loaded down with small children, who might have been happy and reasonably cool at home, struggling desperately to get away for a day in the country, rising at 5 a. m., standing in line at the station, fanning themselves with blasphemy, and weary before they start. We observe them chased home by thunderstorms or colic, dazed and blistered with sunburn, or groaning with a surfeit of ice cream cones.

It is a lamentable fact (and the truth is almost always lamentable, and hotly denied) that for the hard-working majority the week-end is a curse rather than a blessing. The saddest fact in human annals is that most people are never so happy as when they are hard at work. The time may come when criminals will be condemned, not to the chair, but to twenty successive week-ends spent standing in the aisles of crowded excursion trains.

Strolling downtown to a well-known home of fish dinners, it is appetizing to pass along the curve of Dock Street in the coolness of the evening. The clean, lively odours of vegetables and fruit are strong on the air. Under the broad awnings of the commission merchants and produce dealers the stock is piled up in neat and engaging piles ready to be carted away at dawn. Under the glow of pale arcs and gas lamps the colours of the scene are vivid. Great baskets of eggplant shine like huge grapes, a polished port wine colour; green and scarlet peppers catch points of light; a flat pinkish colour gleams on carrots. Each species seems to have an ordered pattern of its own. Potatoes are ranged in a pyramid; watermelons in long rows; white and yellow onions are heaped in sacks. The sweet musk of cantaloupes is the scent that overbreathes all others. Then, down nearer to the waterfront, comes the strong, damp fishy whiff of oysters. To stroll among these gleaming piles of victuals, to watch the various colours where the lamps pour a pale silver and yellow on cairns and pyramids of vegetables, is to gather a lusty appetite and attack the first oyster stew of the season with a stout heart.

It being a very humid day, we stopped to compliment the curly-headed sandwich man at Ninth and Market on his décolleté corsage, which he wears in the Walt Whitman manner. "Wish we could get away with it the way you do," we said, admiringly. He looked at us with the patience of one inured to bourgeois comment. "It's got to be tried," said he, "like everything else."

We stopped by the Weather Man's little illuminated booth at Ninth and Chestnut about 10 o'clock in the evening. We were scrutinizing his pretty coloured pictures, wondering how soon the rain would determine, when a slender young man appeared out of the gloom, said "I'm sorry to have to do this," switched off the light, and pulled down the rolling front of the booth. It was the Weather Man himself.

142

We were greatly elated to meet this mythical sage and walked down the street a little way with him. In order to cheer him up, we complimented him on the artistic charm of his little booth, with its glow of golden light shining on the coloured map and the bright loops and curves of crayon. We told him how almost at any time in the evening groups of people can be seen admiring his stall, but his sensitive heart was gloomy.

"Most of them don't understand it," he said, morosely. "The women are the worst. I've gone there in the evening and found them studying the map eagerly. Hopefully, I would creep up behind to hear their comments. One will say, 'Yes, that's where my husband came from,' or 'I spent last summer over there,' pointing to some place on the map. They seem to think it's put there for them to study geography."

We tried to sympathize with the broken-hearted scientist, but his spirit had been crushed by a long series of woes.

"The other evening," said he, "I saw a couple of girls gazing at the map, and they looked so intelligent I really was charmed. Apparently they were discussing an area of low pressure that was moving down from the Great Lakes, and I lent an ear. Imagine my chagrin when one of them said: 'You see the colour of that chalk line? I'm going to make my next knitted vestee just like that.' And the other one said: 'I think the whole colour scheme is adorable. I'm going to use it as a pattern for my new camouflage bathing-suit.'

"Thank goodness," cried the miserable Weather Man: "I have another map like that down at the Bourse, and the brokers really give it some intelligent attention."

We went on our way sadly, thinking how many sorrows there are in the world. It is grievous to think of the poor Weather Man, lurking with beating pulses in the neighbourhood of Ninth and Chestnut in the hope of finding someone who understands his painstaking display. The next time you are standing in front of his booth do say something about the Oceanic High in the South Atlantic or the dangerous Aleutian Low or the anticyclonic condition prevailing in the Alleghenies. He might overhear you, and it would do his mournful heart good.

It was eight o'clock, a cool drizzling night. Chestnut Street was gray with a dull, pearly, opaque twilight. In the little portico east of

143

Independence Hall the gas lamp under the ceiling cast a soft pink glow on the brick columns.

Independence Square was a sea of tremulous, dripping boughs. The quaint heptahedral lamps threw splashed shimmers of topaz colour across the laky pavement. "Golden lamps in a green night," as Marvell says, twinkled through the stir and moisture of the evening.

ON GOING TO BED

One of the characters in "The Moon and Sixpence" remarked that he had faithfully lived up to the old precept about doing every day two things you heartily dislike; for, said he, every day he had got up and he had gone to bed.

It is a sad thing that as soon as the hands of the clock have turned ten the shadow of going to bed begins to creep over the evening. We have never heard bedtime spoken of with any enthusiasm. One after another we have seen a gathering disperse, each person saying (with an air of solemn resignation): "Well, I guess I'll go to bed." But there was no hilarity about it. It is really rather touching how they cling to the departing skirts of the day that is vanishing under the spinning shadow of night.

This is odd, we repeat, for sleep is highly popular among human beings. The reluctance to go to one's couch is not at all a reluctance to slumber, for almost all of us will doze happily in an armchair or on a sofa, or even festooned on the floor with a couple of cushions. But the actual and formal yielding to sheets and blankets is to be postponed to the last possible moment.

The devil of drowsiness is at his most potent, we find, about 10:30 p. m. At this period the human carcass seems to consider that it has finished its cycle, which began with so much courage nearly sixteen hours before. It begins to slack and the mind halts on a dead centre every now and then, refusing to complete the revolution. Now there are those who hold that this is certainly the seemly and appointed time to go to bed and they do so as a matter of routine. These are, commonly, the happier creatures, for they take the tide of sleep at the flood and are borne calmly and with gracious gentleness out to great waters of nothingness. They push off from the wharf on a tranquil current and nothing more is to be seen or heard of these voyagers until they reappear at the breakfast table, digging lustily into their grape fruit.

These people are happy, aye, in a brutish and sedentary fashion, but they miss the admirable adventures of those more embittered wrestlers who will not give in without a struggle. These latter suffer severe pangs between 10:30 and about 11:15 while they grapple with their fading faculties and seek to reëstablish the will on its tottering throne. This requires courage stout, valour unbending. Once you yield, be it ever so little, to the tempter, you are lost. And here our poor barren clay plays us false, undermining the intellect with many a trick and wile. "I will sit down for a season in that comfortable chair," the creature says to himself, "and read this sprightly novel. That will ease my mind and put me in humour for a continuance of lively thinking." And the end of that man is a steady nasal buzz from the bottom of the chair where he has collapsed, an unsightly object and a disgrace to humanity. This also means a big bill from the electric light company at the end of the month. In many such ways will his corpus bewray him, leading him by plausible self-deceptions into a pitfall of sleep, whence he is aroused about 3 a. m. when the planet turns over on the other side. Only by stiff perseverance and rigid avoidance of easy chairs may the critical hour between 10:30 and 11:30 be safely passed. Tobacco, a self-brewed pot of tea, and a browsing along bookshelves (remain standing and do not sit down with your book) are helps in this time of struggle. Even so, there are some happily drowsy souls who can never cross these shallows alone without grounding on the Lotus Reefs. Our friend J—— D—— K——, magnificent creature, was (when we lived with him) so potently hypnoidal that, even erect and determined as his bookcase and urgently bent upon Brann's Iconoclast or some other literary irritant, sleep would seep through his pores and he would fall with a crash, lying there in unconscious bliss until someone came in and prodded him up, reeling and ashamed.

But, as we started to say, those who survive this drastic weeding out which Night imposes upon her wooers—so as to cull and choose only the truly meritorious lovers—experience supreme delights which are unknown to their snoring fellows. When the struggle with somnolence has been fought out and won, when the world is all-covering darkness and close-pressing silence, when the tobacco suddenly takes on fresh vigour and fragrance and the books lie strewn about the table, then it seems as though all the rubbish and floating matter of the day's thoughts have poured away and only the bright, clear, and swift current of the mind itself remains, flowing happily and without impediment. This perfection of existence is not to be reached very often; but when properly approached it may be won. It is a different mind that one uncovers then, a spirit which is lucid and hopeful, to which (for a few serene hours) time exists not. The friable resolutions of the day are brought out again and recemented and chiselled anew. Surprising schemes are started and carried through to happy conclusion, lifetimes of amazement are lived in a few passing ticks. There is one who at such moments resolves, with complete sincerity, to start at one end of the top shelf

146

and read again all the books in his library, intending this time really to extract their true marrow. He takes a clean sheet of paper and sets down memoranda of all the people he intends to write to, and all the plumbers and what not that he will call up the next day. And the next time this happy seizure attacks him he will go through the same gestures again without surprise and without the slightest mortification. And then, having lived a generation of good works since midnight struck, he summons all his resolution and goes to bed.

The End

9 781647 996871